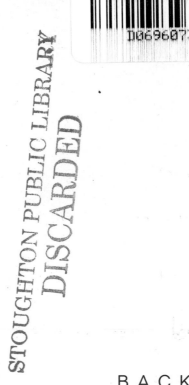
BACK
TALK

B A C K

T A L K

alex richards

Woodbury, Minnesota

First Edition
First Printing, 2007

Book design by Steffani Chambers and Joanna Willis
Cover design by Ellen Dahl
Cover photo © 2006 by Nicolas Russell / Riser / Getty Images

Flux, an imprint of Llewellyn Publications

Library of Congress Cataloging-in-Publication Data
Richards, Alex, 1979
  Back Talk / Alex Richards.—1st ed.
    p. cm.
  Summary: Small town, sixteen-year-old Gemma comes to New York City to do a summer internship for Kate Morgan's talk show, only to have her eyes opened at some of the hard realities within the career field.
  ISBN 978-0-7387-1017-4
  [1. Friendship—Fiction. 2. Television programs—Fiction. 3. Coming of age—Fiction. 4. New York (N.Y.)—Fiction.] I. Title.
  PZ7.R3783Bac 2007
  [Fic]—dc22
                                                              2007004507

Flux
A Division of Llewellyn Worldwide, Ltd.
2143 Wooddale Drive, Dept. 978-0-7387-1017-4
Woodbury, MN 55125-2989, U.S.A.
www.fluxnow.com

Printed in the United States of America

Acknowledgments

I would like to give special thanks to Julie Culver for helping me rework this book and making it sellable (and then selling it!). Thank you also to Andrew Karre and Karl Anderson at Flux for all their brilliant ideas. A big shout-out to all my TV-industry peeps—this book wouldn't exist without you guys—and most importantly, to my parents, my sister, and my brand-new husband for their tireless support and encouragement.

To my mom, Claudia,
the supernova of brilliance.

ONE

"Metallic or electric blue?"

Gemma sighed painfully, looking over at Dana's latest monumental wardrobe crisis. "Metallic."

Dana narrowed her deep green eyes at Gemma. "Do you *really* like the metallic shirt better or are you just saying that so I'll shut up? Because if you—"

"Jeez, Dana!" Gemma exploded. She flopped down on the bed, pretending to strangle herself.

Poor Gemma. A closet fit was one thing, but helping Dana was like prepping Lindsay Lohan for the Academy Awards. Dana needed Steven Cojocaru, not Gemma Winters. The words "fashion advice" and "Gemma" were as mismatched as post-laundry-day socks, but her enthusiasm was charming, in a Forrest Gump sort of way.

"Dana, the metallic shirt is cute. So was the sexy green sweater you showed me five minutes ago, and the gray-and-white Chloe tunic you tried on ten minutes before that. The only one I didn't like was that green burlap dress. I know it's vintage or whatever, but it looked like you found that thing in a Dumpster and it should have stayed there. Sorry."

"Fine."

Dana discarded the electric blue camisole by throwing it at Gemma's head and hung the metallic blouse over the closet door. Wise choice. Electric blue made Dana look like Smurfette on meth. The silk camisole slid off Gemma's shoulder, crumpling in a heap on the hardwood floor. She couldn't help but wonder if Dana was subconsciously using *her* as a laundry basket—the fashion elite so often blur the lines between friend and assistant.

Gemma bent down, tossing the shirt into the actual laundry hamper and grabbed the June issue of *Cosmo* in exchange. Hot-date closet fits are never fun for the dateless friend, and Gemma had had enough. In her sixteen years on earth, she could count her entire dating history on one hand, and watching leggy, blonde Dana Cox prepare for yet another night on the town just rubbed it in. Gemma could read every article in every *Cosmo* and still not get a guy. Skimming the pages, she paused on "How to Have Great Solo Sex" and sighed.

But Gemma Winters had plenty to keep her busy this summer without having to worry about her G spot or scoring a hot date. She was living in glamorous, exciting, heart-pounding New York City, and she'd snagged a totally enviable internship at one of the hippest daytime talk shows: *Back Talk with Kate Morgan.* The show was total cheese but completely addictive. It was Gemma's dream job. Well, more like a pit stop on the road to her dream career. *And* it got her out of Ketchum, Idaho: Hometown from Hell.

Seriously, it was the dream setup—the kind they make reality TV shows about. Step aside, *The Hills*, and make way for three girls taking New York by storm. Imagine the possibilities. There's Gemma, the girl next door brimming with Midwestern naïveté and spending the summer before her senior year hobnobbing with the most powerful execs in television.

And what boosts ratings better than gorgeous millionaire sidekicks? Dana Cox and fellow boarding school inmate America Vanderbilt fill the *Lifestyles of the Rich and Famous* angle. America is the world-weary, been-there-done-that heiress escaping her stuffy life in Boston to intern at her parents' ritzy auction house. And Dana, the aspiring actress, has a lengthy to-do list including but not limited to throwing a few ragers in her wicked stepmother's giant, practically unsupervised townhouse. She also has the sticky task of acquainting corn-fed Gemma with purebred America, but if they both like Dana "the black sheep" Cox, they can all bond over a little ready-for-prime-time delinquent behavior.

At the moment, the black sheep was standing in front of a full-length mirror, lacing up a sexy silk bustier with matching white panties. The white silk looked fluorescent against Dana's tan skin. She gave her reflection a sultry wink and a smile, no doubt admiring the 34Cs she got for her sixteenth birthday.

Gemma peeked her head up from *Cosmo* and blushed. "You're not *really* going to wear that, are you?" she asked. "I mean, the guy's not going to see it, *right?*"

Blatantly risqué was so not Gemma.

"I don't know, *Dad*," Dana replied. "But a girl's got a right to feel like a sex bomb. And god forbid, if I die tonight, I don't want the NYPD to see me in cotton skivvies. When the good lord takes me, it's gonna be in Cartier and Agent Provocateur."

"God, Dana! Thanks for the visual," Gemma laughed.

"It's my plesh-uh," Dana drawled, batting her fake lashes. She unhooked the bustier and tossed it on the floor, delving back into a ransacked underwear drawer. She'd vetoed her teddies from La Perla and tacky Victoria's Secret pushup bras and commandeered America's room to check out her selection. America had brought enough luggage to open a Barney's Co-op out of her bedroom, although it would be slim pickings for anyone above a size four. That meant Gemma. She had more of an hourglass figure, though it crept up to an hour and a half if she bailed on the gym too often.

"White Prada skirt or Marc Jacobs mini?"

"You are driving me crazy!" Gemma screamed, pulling at her long wavy brown hair. "Dana, tomorrow is my first day of work. I should be having my own closet fit! Seriously, all my nice clothes are wool. I don't want to die of heatstroke but I'll look like an idiot teenager if I wear a crappy Target sundress."

"Do you really shop at *Target*?" Dana asked. It seemed wrong to Dana to buy clothes where Cheez Whiz and fishing tackle were sold. "Never mind," she added with a dismissive wave. "You're *sixteen*, of course you're an idiot teenager!"

"Oh! I'm sorry, Grandma! Does the Mensa membership come with the seventeenth birthday card, or should I just expect a cake in two months?"

Touchy, touchy.

"I was just kidding," Dana groaned. "We already picked an outfit that you're totally going to rock, so stop freaking out. You're gonna be an awesome intern. And if you fuck it up, don't worry. I know my washed-up stepbitch got you the job, but she's not going to give a shit if you quit or get fired."

Dana's maternal instinct was somewhat lacking.

Gemma tossed *Cosmo* on the floor and stomped toward America's door, pouting a little. This internship was a *huge* deal to her. Not only had Reese Cox put in a good word for her with the executive producer of *Back Talk*, she'd also let Gemma and America move into her palatial Upper West Side brownstone. Mrs. Cox spent five minutes a year there, but Gemma didn't know that (and more importantly neither did her parents), and she didn't want to get on the woman's bad side.

Dana was just bitter because her stepmother paid absolutely *no* attention to her. Forgotten birthdays, re-shoots in

Toronto on Christmas—the life of an abandoned celebutante. That was how Gemma and Dana became friends in the first place. Mrs. Cox went totally AWOL on a mother/daughter bonding trip to Sun Valley. The Winters family had adopted Dana while the former *Melrose Place* regular hit the slopes and schmoozed with actors and producers over hot toddies in the ski lodge.

"One more teensy favor, Gem?" Dana asked, struggling to balance between a black Chanel pump and a metallic Missoni wedge.

"The black one, asshole," Gemma added, only half annoyed. "Have fun on your date. Come say hi if you get in early."

"Don't count on it!"

Gemma shut the door behind her, dragging her feet down the cool oak hallway to her bedroom. She couldn't believe Dana picked *tonight* to go on a date with some random guy from Blockbuster. Even America, who Gemma had only known for a day, checked before making plans. Not that Gemma asked her to stay. How pathetic would that have looked? No, Gemma decided she could brave a night alone in the apartment.

Chinese take-out in front of a TV the size of Texas? Rough life.

Popping Fiona Apple into the CD player, Gemma grabbed a ruffly, decorative pillow from the bed and hugged it to her chest. She was starting to freak out a little. Every time she heard a car horn or a police siren—which is, like, every seven seconds in New York—she nearly jumped out of her skin. Thinking about her trek to work the next morning scared her more than she cared to admit, not to mention how she'd survive once she got there. Her previous job of renting out skis hadn't exactly prepared her for network TV.

She needed someone to calm her down. Forget Dana and America. She didn't want to talk to them anyway. Maybe Gabriella, the Cox's housekeeper, would have some words of wisdom. Not likely, since the woman barely spoke English, but Gemma thought she was sweet. She said "¡Ay, dios mío!" a lot and smelled like rosemary.

Gemma wound her way down three flights of stairs and through a metal door to Gabriella's garden apartment. The house was a maze. How could they possibly need two dozen rooms, what with Dana off at boarding school, her stepbrother, Danny, in Japan becoming the next Donald Trump, and Mrs. Cox constantly jet-setting?

Gemma obviously didn't watch *Cribs*.

"¿Hola, Gabriella?" Gemma said, knocking loudly to be heard over the TV. Gabriella was addicted to some cheesy soap called *Gitanas*, which Dana described as Mexico's answer to *Charmed*. "Es Gemma. ¿Entro, por favor?"

Gemma's Spanish sucked.

"¡Por supuesto, Gemma!" Gabriella called out from behind the door. She pronounced Gemma's name with a hard *G* instead of the *J* sound she was used to, but it wasn't worth correcting.

"Sorry to bother you. I mean, *lo siento*," Gemma said, entering the spacious living room. "I just thought I'd come and say hi."

Gemma perched on the edge of the chair next to Gabriella, mesmerized by the old woman's tiny tanned fingers weaving colorful yarn on a hand-held loom. The repetition was soothing for about thirty seconds until swelling panic hit Gemma again. She tried to breathe steadily, but she was on the verge of tears.

"You go to new work tomorrow, Gemma?" Gabriella asked patiently.

"Yes, and I'm petrified. I think I'm going to have a panic attack!" Gemma exhaled heavily, suppressing the urge to vomit. The flickering votive candles on Gabriella's dresser were starting to give her a migraine. "What if I can't find the right office when I get to the building? Or I break the copy machine? I know I'm going to break something. Everyone's going to think I'm a total fashion victim—Dana already does. Ugh, I'm *so* not cut out for this. What if they fire me on the spot?"

"¡Dios mío!" Gabriella laughed. She pulled her graying brown hair to the left of her neck and twisted it into a braid. "Dana say you work very hard. And you like this TV program, no?"

Gemma nodded. Who doesn't like trashy TV? "This spring I downloaded an episode log of all four seasons," she admitted. It had taken her a week to look through it all. "I'm kind of addicted." And kind of a stalker!

"Kate Morgan used to be a movie star," Gemma said, relaxing a little. She was like an encyclopedia of random entertainment trivia, but Gabriella didn't seem to mind. "She stopped acting because she got breast cancer. I think she started the talk show to raise awareness after she went into remission."

"I think I seen it," Gabriella said, weaving methodically. "She interview celebrities, too, no?"

"Yeah. Did you see when she had Drew Barrymore on last week? She got Drew to show her—" Gemma paused, giggling nervously. She was crossing the lines of appropriate conversation with the fifty-something Mexican woman.

Gemma sighed and twisted a simple silver bracelet around her wrist. "I'm scared I'll mess up."

"You gonna do fine, mi niña." Gabriella put her loom down and looked deep into Gemma's eyes. Finally, the sage advice Gemma had been waiting for. "When I first come to Nueva York, fifteen years ago, I am so scared! Pero, Señor Cox, he take me in." Gabriella paused to kiss the crucifix around her neck and cross herself. She did that every time she mentioned Dana's dead father. "It is hard to live in a new place, but look." Gabriella pointed to a row of pictures on the dresser. There were a few creepy pictures of Jesus, some old family photos, and Dana's latest headshot. "I send money to mi familia en Mexico, and I watch Dana grow up here. Everything is okay for me, and you going to be okay, too."

"Thanks, Gabriella."

Gemma got up and walked to the door, leaving Gabriella to weave and watch *Gitanas* in peace. "Good night. Hasta mañana."

"Si. ¡Buena suerte!"

It was nice talking to Gabriella. Depressing, but nice. Gemma pulled the door shut and trudged back upstairs, embarrassed to admit that she missed her family. How could she be homesick after two days in New York? Most sixteen-year-olds would kill for this kind of freedom. She pulled her cell phone out of her pocket and started dialing. *I'll just call home for a second.* Her parents' obnoxious, lecturing voices would surely knock the homesickness right out of her.

"Yo," answered a wobbly male voice after the third ring.

"Excuse me?" Gemma laughed. "Since when do you say 'Yo'? Suddenly my little brother thinks he's Ludacris."

"Hey, G! I thought you were Tina."

Derek Winters: pint-sized playa'.

"Who's Tina?"

Derek sighed. "If you're gonna be gone all summer, you can't expect to be up-to-date on my love life."

"I've been gone for *two* days." *You little brat.* "You're turning into quite the little pimp, aren't you? I didn't think fourteen-year-old boys even *liked* girls. Don't they still have cooties?"

"Screw you! Tina's a *cheerleader*," Derek said. Alert the media.

"Ooh," Gemma wowed. "A cheerleader dating the captain of the JV basketball team? Your babies will be flexible meathead hybrids."

"Eat shit and die, you sicko retard," he shot back at her. Feel the love. "So, what's up? Does *Back Talk* start tomorrow?"

"Uh-huh." Gemma lay on her bed tracing the ornate molding on the ceiling with her eyes. The whole room had kind of a Versailles thing going on. "I was hoping for a little guidance. Where are the olds?"

"Out. Dad drove Mom to some veterinarian conference, but I'll tell you what she'd say: 'Just be yourself and everyone will love you.'" Derek's imitation of their mother's Midwestern accent was hilarious. "Dad would tell you some boring-ass story about his first job doing ski boot repairs and you'd fall asleep. My advice," he offered, "is to get Stephon Marbury on the show and get his autograph for me."

"I'm guessing that's a basketball player," Gemma said flatly. She couldn't fault him for being fourteen. "Thanks for your support, dumb-ass. I'll talk to you later. Oh, and good luck with Tina."

"Thanks." He paused, then added, "Kick some *Back Talk* ass this summer so it's worth the pain you've caused your family."

"Aw, that almost sounded sincere," Gemma cooed. "I miss you, too, punk."

She pressed END and reached across the four-poster bed, connecting her phone to its charger. Derek was a little prick, but he cheered her up. Gemma sighed. Finally there was nothing standing in the way of her and a lonely night of self-pity. She shimmied into her favorite Gap PJs and walked down one flight of stairs to the Informal Den. Some millionaires feel the need to label rooms. It can get *so* confusing otherwise.

Gemma flopped down on one of three oversized suede sofas and grabbed the remotes from the glass coffee table. The straight-to-video action movie was in the DVD player and the fat-free popcorn was popped. All she had to do now was *not* think about *Back Talk with Kate Morgan* . . . like *that* was possible.

TWO

Gemma's hand quivered as she brought the mascara to her eye.

"Calm *down*," she scolded her reflection.

Gemma was a mess—crack addicts have more composure. Her laundry list of setbacks started with a restless night's sleep; hair so big she could have won a Miss Texas pageant; and an evil, top-of-the-line coffee maker that she just couldn't figure out. She'd counted on a strong cup before wielding the mascara wand, but sadly defeated, she had to finish her morning ritual uncaffeinated.

She pulled her frizzy brown tornado of hair into a tight ponytail, accentuating her chubby, Cabbage Patch Kid cheeks. But the outfit was cute: a baby blue, cashmere T-shirt; black capri pants; and Manolo heels, courtesy of America. Gemma thought the top made her arms look flabby, but we all have our crosses to bear, and it was a far cry from her Target threads. The whole outfit was way too dressy for Idaho, but Dana assured her it was standard style for Manhattan.

Gemma threw the mascara onto the white marble floor of the bathroom. Okay, so the makeup thing wasn't going to happen today. She put on a little sheer Clinique lipstick in Black Honey and gave her reflection a judgmental once-over. Was this a funhouse fat mirror? Gemma sighed. Maybe if the internship didn't work out she could always dance backup for Sir Mix-A-Lot. She could deal with the rest of her curves—everything but the butt. She picked up her green canvas beach bag and began the descent down to the kitchen. With any luck, climbing two flights of stairs to her bedroom all summer would give her buns of steel.

"Don't you look snappy this morning," America commented as Gemma walked into the kitchen.

America was sitting at the breakfast table reading Camus—in *French*—in a red silk Takashimaya kimono. Her disheveled French twist screamed casual elegance, and was that a *silver spoon* she used to daintily shovel honeydew into her mouth? She was *such* a China doll. She looked like Mischa Barton, although America wasn't out of control like Marissa on *The O.C.* Even now, after three key lime martinis at last night's Whitney Museum benefit, she was dewy, composed, and alert. Gemma suspected America had a masseuse chained up in her bedroom.

"Thanks again for the shoes. They're so awesome," Gemma gushed. She anxiously scanned the kitchen. This was her first one-on-one with America and she didn't know what to say. The weather, favorite book, …*some*thing.

"Are you starting your internship today?" Gemma finally asked.

"Mmm, I thought I might swing by later," America replied breezily.

Oh *might* she?

America didn't need to work a day in her life if she didn't want to. With a name like America Vanderbilt, isn't it obvious that she was rich? She wasn't, like, a *Vanderbilt* Vanderbilt—aren't they all broke anyway?—but her family was definitely made of money. The auction house thing was more like the *Cliff's Notes* version of an internship. It appeased her parents and jazzed up her college applications.

Gemma smiled blankly. How could America be so blasé about work?

"Coffee?" America asked. "I'm going to make a fresh pot."

"*Definitely*," Gemma said. Her lack thereof was starting to give her the shakes. "Can I toast you an English muffin?"

"Just a half, thanks," America responded politely.

Gemma reached into the chrome breadbox for English muffins and slid one and a half into the toaster while America casually flipped the switch on the stainless steel coffee maker. Instantly the machine rumbled and hissed, the aroma of fresh-brewed Blue Mountain wafting across the room. *That* was the evil coffee maker?

Gemma glared at the stainless steal traitor. "I *hate* machines. Is it possible to be cursed by an appliance?" She sighed, fidgeting with the "Vote for Pedro" pin on her bag. "It's just a matter of time before I break something at work. I wish I lived in the olden days. *Before* technology."

"Dana was right," America observed. "You're incredibly neurotic."

Gemma blushed. She knew she was neurotic, and she knew that *Dana* knew she was neurotic, but America made it sound so ... *annoying.* But that was just America being America. Her tone often lacked the subtlety it had in her head.

"Don't go back to the olden days," America said, pulling two antique floral mugs from a cupboard. "I don't think they bathed much back then and all the knights had greasy long hair. And would you want to wear a chastity belt?" She made an icky face.

"Good point!" Gemma giggled as the toaster pinged. She got out two plates and handed the less-burnt English muffin to America.

"And just because I said 'olden days,'" Gemma continued, slathering raspberry jam on her muffin, "doesn't necessarily mean *medieval.* Maybe I want to be in Jane Austen land, practicing needlepoint and having an earth-shattering romance."

"Those guys weren't much for hygiene, either," America said. "But seriously, don't be nervous about today. I think you're going to be fine. And if something breaks, blame somebody else!"

"That's the kind of thing Dana would say."

"We're rich," America shrugged. "We never learned the whole 'actions have consequences' thing."

For all her harsh overtones, America had a pretty decent sense of humor. Dana had described her as funny but as far as first impressions go, America was about as funny as a lampshade. But just look at the two of them: Gemma and America making each other breakfast and chitchatting away. If they kept it up, they'd be BFF in no time.

When her coffee had cooled, Gemma gulped it down with a little skim milk and put her empty plate and cup into the dishwasher.

"I'm off to work!" she announced. She popped an Altoid in her mouth and ran her tongue along her top teeth, checking for food. "I clocked it yesterday and it took me twenty minutes door-to-door. See you tonight?"

"Mmhm," America smiled. She tore off a morsel of English muffin and popped it in her mouth as if she were nursing a sick bird back to health. "I'll probably go shopping this afternoon. If work's horrible, feel free to join me at Bergdorf's."

"Yeah *right*." Gemma laughed, mistaking America's offer for a joke.

She grabbed her bag and walked out onto Eighty-Third Street. The hot summer sun warmed her skin instantly. Gemma had yet to experience the truly excruciating New York humidity. She pulled her cheap drugstore shades out of her bag and walked toward the subway station.

The subway platform at Eighty-First Street was packed. Gemma looked down at her crappy Timex and cursed under her breath. The New York Newbie didn't realize that "clocking it" meant virtually nothing. *Everyone* knows you can't predict the subway.

She took a tissue out of her bag, mopping beads of sweat off her forehead. If it was 90 degrees outside, it had to be at least 100 in the dank underground pit.

"Great. A heat wave," Gemma mumbled to herself.

"Just Mother Nature fucking with us."

Gemma stiffened at the sound of a man's voice behind her. Poor girl, she probably thought she'd get mugged on the spot. Everything about her from those bright brown eyes to her dorky canvas bag screamed, *I'm from out of town! Beat me up and take all my money!*

She tightened her grip on her bag and peered onto the tracks, casually inching her way down the platform. It was hard resisting the overwhelming urge to turn and look at the guy, but her father's voice warning her, "You give 'em an inch and they take a mile!" echoed in her head. She couldn't give this creep the satisfaction.

A whoosh of warm air (and a wave of relief) rushed over Gemma as the dull yellow headlights of the C train came into the station. Fear made a temporary New Yorker out of Gemma as she elbowed her way on like a linebacker and grabbed the nearest handrail for stability. It was like qualifying for the New Yorker Olympics. She pressed her lips tightly together, taking quick breaths through her nose while visions of anthrax danced in her head. If Gemma actually knew how many germs there were in New York City, she'd probably be on the first plane back to Idaho.

As crowded and smelly as the subway was, Gemma found it kind of cool. This was *New York City*—home to eight million people from busboys to billionaires. She looked around the rest of the car trying to guess what everyone did. Briefcase lady with the power-perm had to be a lawyer. To her left she was immediately entranced with a cute guy in a tattered blue button-down shirt with the cuffs rolled up. He had a Jonathan-Rhys-Meyers-circa-*Bend-It-Like-Beckham* thing going on. Yummy.

His deep brown eyes brightened when he noticed Gemma staring. She quickly turned away. *Don't stare at him, idiot*, she ordered, but her eyes levitated back in his direction anyway. He stuffed his copy of *Crime and Punishment* into a threadbare mailbag and smiled.

Ooh, a possible subway tryst. How exciting.

Gemma gripped her bag with both hands as the subway doors swung open and swarms of people pushed past her. She inappropriately squeezed her eyes shut and grabbed onto a handrail, praying for survival as she waited for the doors to shut again.

"Sorry."

Gemma pried one eye open, curious to see who was apologizing. It was the cute Jonathan Rhys Meyers guy—and he was standing right next to her. She couldn't believe how close he was. So close that she could smell his shampoo. It was something sweet, like pears or almonds. And what was he apologizing for? Certainly not his sizzling hot good looks.

"I didn't mean to scare you with my 'Mother Nature' comment."

Gemma gasped. *This* was creepy-subway-platform guy? Why do the cute ones always have to be psychos? She bit her lip, not sure whether to scream or spit in his face, when the subway pulled into the Fifty-Ninth Street station.

Gemma booked it off the train, stopping dizzily on the platform to get her bearings. She gulped to relieve her cottonmouth then looked back into the train. Subway Guy *still* smiling at her. He gave her a mini-salute and the train pulled out of the station and into darkness. Was that *it*? She didn't know whether to praise the lord or burst into tears.

BACK TALK

A chill went up Gemma's spine as she walked into the impressive thirty-story building. Everything from the news to home shopping shows had been produced in this building for over fifty years. She picked up her new ID badge and walked to the elevators, secretly getting a thrill from the sound of her Manolos echoing against the floor. This was it. In a matter of minutes, Gemma Winters would be An Intern. She felt like "First Day of Work" Barbie.

She walked down the long, beige corridor on the twenty-third floor toward frosted glass doors. Gemma loved the curvy chick-lit font of the *Back Talk with Kate Morgan* logo stenciled across them. It screamed feminine midlife crisis. She tightened her ponytail and took a deep, confidence-inducing breath.

The reception area was decorated in mid-century modern—not that Gemma would have known that. The funky, uncomfortable-looking red plastic chairs and stiff chrome and leather Le Corbusier sofa were like nothing she'd ever seen. It wasn't quite how Gemma had pictured it. For one thing, the room was kind of deserted. The receptionist was the only person in there, and she was watching TV. Gemma put her bag down on a low, black-lacquered table and walked up to the front desk.

"Hi," Gemma said. She folded her arms across her chest, then quickly unfolded them. She rested her hands on her hips but it made her look too defiant so she just let them dangle by her sides. Oh. My. *God.*

"I'm Gemma Winters. One of the new interns?" Her voice cracked.

The pretty, twenty-something black girl looked up from the TV and smiled. "Hey, Gemma! That's a cool name by the way. I'm Melissa, the receptionist until they promote my ass." She extended a well-manicured hand for Gemma to shake while twirling her long, silky black hair with the other.

"Welcome to KM. That's what we call it around here," Melissa said. "Did you have trouble getting past security?"

"No," Gemma lied. The security guards had been total pricks. They made her dig up two forms of ID and joked that she looked too young to be in "the biz."

"Good. Those guys are jerks," Melissa huffed. "They're always up in my face. I think they're overcompensating for something." Melissa wiggled her pinky finger in the air and laughed.

Melissa was a total New Yorker. Not the aggressive, eye-contact-avoiding kind of New Yorker Gemma's mother had warned her about, but the friendly, compassionate kind. Gemma had been freaking out over nothing. What a surprise.

"Grab a seat, Gemma. I'll find a PA to give you a tour."

Gemma noticed a selection of magazines on the coffee table—*Marie Claire, Jane, Time, U.S. News & World Report*—but she was too jittery to read. Once her ears picked up on the whir of phones, faxes, and muddled conversations, it started to feel a lot more "bustling" to her. This was a *real* office.

"Are you Gemma?"

The guy standing in front of her looked more like a football player than a talk show producer, but Gemma had nothing whatsoever to base her opinion on. At the very least he looked more L.A. than N.Y. He shoved his hands in his pockets as he gave her a "what up" nod.

"I'm Bobby McKinsey. I guess I'm going to show you around."

Try not to sound so excited, Bobby.

Gemma followed him amiably, trying not to laugh at his affected white-boy homie walk. There was something endearing about Bobby. He reminded her of her little brother, Derek. Not that she'd ever tell *him* that.

"I guess there's not really a dress code?" Gemma asked, noticing the Abercrombie & Fitch-ness of Bobby's baggy khakis and striped polo shirt. Suddenly her oh-so-strategically-planned outfit felt oh-so-retarded.

"Not so much," Bobby shrugged. "At least, not up here. But on tape-days you have to be down on the floor with guests. Then you gotta tighten your game."

Down on the floor with guests? Gemma thought in horror. It had to be office lingo because wrestling on the floor with strangers sounded too weird. Not that Bobby bothered to explain. Bobby was a real prize.

He turned left at the first door they came to and led Gemma into a large room with a picture window looking out onto another building. Four young women sat at desks, typing frantically on their Macs and jabbering into headsets. The air smelled of stale Glade Plug-Ins.

"Hey ladies. We got a new intern."

Bobby and Gemma waited for acknowledgement, but the only response came from a bored-looking black girl with caramel extensions and tacky acrylic nails. All the other girls were practically making out with their computers.

"That's Carla," Bobby said. "And there's Stacy, Kamara, and Val. Carla and Val are APs. That's short for associate producer. Stacy and Kamara are researchers.

"It's like a pyramid. Penelope O'Shea is the EP. Below her are the other execs and supervisors. Then producers, and then APs, and then researchers," Bobby said, counting off the hierarchy on his stubby fingers. "At the bottom of the barrel are production assistants. And way down below *that* are the interns."

"So I've got the real glamorous job?"

Gemma's sarcasm went cruelly unnoticed judging by the look on Bobby's face. Oh well. It was pretty clear Bobby and Gemma weren't MFEO, so who cared what comedic style he preferred?

"You'll have to do tons of shit for the APs," Bobby complained. "Like research articles and make phone calls. It's so boring."

Bobby sounded like a robot. How *Stepford Wives* of him. He pulled Gemma back into the hallway and steered her toward another roomful of computers and savvy employees. This time the response was much peppier. Gemma blushed as everyone stopped and stared at her. Fresh meat.

"Yo. We got a new intern," Bobby said, pointing at Gemma.

"Nina," said an older woman in thick, tortoise-rimmed glasses.

"I'm Simone. I'm the production coordinator. We spoke on the phone a few weeks ago." Gemma smiled and nodded. Finally a familiar name. "I'll be giving you some of your more boring assignments. Inventory and restock, mostly." Simone was incredibly well dressed. More high fashion than corporate, though. She looked like a model with porcelain skin and perfectly blown-out blonde locks. Gemma would die if she knew that Simone's haircut cost more than an iPod.

"That's James." Bobby gestured toward a well-built guy with weathered movie-star good looks and a greasy salt-and-pepper 'do.

"Finch … James Finch."

Loser … Total Loser.

"Welcome to KM. I'm a producer, so you'd better do whatever I say." James flashed a salacious toothy grin.

Gemma bit her lip to keep from laughing. James was the real life Deuce Bigalow.

"Hey kid, I'm just messing with you," he chuckled with a wink. "I *am* a producer, but you don't have to do whatever I say. Unless I ask … but nothing kinky," he teased devilishly.

Congratulations, Gemma: meet your first smarmy old letch.

A short, busty blonde swatted James on the shoulder. "You're going to get fired for saying shit like that." Her shrill Long Island accent pierced Gemma's ears. "Hi, I'm Deniece, also a producer."

"Hi," Gemma squeaked, looking down at her hands. "I'm pleased meet you."

"Look how cute and polite she is," Deniece shrieked condescendingly. "But, duty calls. I've got to pre-interview a child molester at ten."

Gemma's head sprang to attention. Interview a *what*? With a wave, she watched Deniece, James, Simone, and Nina head out of the room. Producers, she discovered, made her nervous. Somewhat more relaxed, she rocked back and forth on her heels, checking out the two guys sitting around drinking coffee. The younger one was H-O-Triple-T, and Gemma blushed immediately. He looked twenty-ish and *very* doable. The other guy looked nice, but his matted blonde poodle-fro wasn't doing it for her.

"I'm Nick Daltrey," the cute one said, putting his hand on his chest.

He was very Swedish tennis pro, but Gemma couldn't get enough.

"Hi," she said, batting her lashes as she gently twirled the end of her ponytail.

Subtle.

"Hello, Gemma! It's nice to meet you. I'm Haden," the other, older guy boomed.

Gemma giggled. Haden sounded exactly like Mr. Moviefone.

Bobby sighed heavily. "Anyway, Haden's our graphic designer and Nick's his intern. Graphics is on the ninth floor so you might not see them much."

Bummer, Gemma thought, waving goodbye as they walked out of the room. With an ass like that, bumping into Nick around the water cooler would have been fun.

BACK TALK

"Oh. My. God. It's Sydney Bristow!"

Gemma looked quizzically at the cute black guy standing in the doorway. Was he talking to her? She'd been faxing video footage requests for over two hours and her perception skills were ... well, they *weren't*. The room she was holed up in—affectionately dubbed "Hell"—was sucking the life out of her and she had a pretty good idea why. It had to do with the hierarchy Bobby had mentioned. Producers got big, bright offices to themselves, APs and researchers shared big, bright offices, and PAs and interns were stuck in Hell with no windows, no ventilation, and no TV.

"Don't you think?" he asked, his arms crossed over his chest expectantly.

The guy was well dressed. Possibly too well dressed to be straight, but Gemma couldn't be sure and wasn't about to ask. Questioning a guy's sexual preference in the first five minutes of conversation? Not the best way to make new friends, even for a newbie from the sticks.

Gemma looked around the empty room and back at the guy.

"Girl, you look like *Alias*!" he squealed. "*Alias*," he said louder and slower, the way you'd talk to a German tourist. "Am I the only one who watched that show? No wonder it got cancelled," he sighed dramatically. "You totally look like Jennifer Garner."

"*Ohhh.*" Gemma laughed. *Jennifer Garner when she was preggers.*

"Sorry," she said, lightly swatting her temples. "I get mental menopause sometimes."

"Mental menopause," he giggled. "I *love* it!"

"Thanks," Gemma giggled back. How *adorable* was this guy? And the jury was in: definitely gay. She took a step back and looked him up and down. "And you look like...Theo Huxtable."

His eyes widened. "Get *out*! I used to want to *be* Theo Huxtable! Then I decided I'd rather be Denise, but that's a different story. I'm Clark."

"Kent?" Gemma snorted. "Bad joke, sorry. I'm Gemma Winters. The new intern."

Clark's face soured. "Ouch. An intern. Well, everyone's got to pay their dues, I guess. I'm Kate's assistant."

"Kate *Morgan*?" Gemma asked, her eyes sparkling with awe. "Do you totally love her?"

Clark's plastic smile said it all.

He spent the next hour telling Gemma his life story, from majoring in communications at Northwestern to interning at a failed sitcom—remember *Second Time Around*? Neither did Gemma.

"But I secretly want to be an anchor on *Access Hollywood*," he added with a devilish grin.

In terms of "office gossip" he didn't divulge much, but alluded to a few intra-office romances. He warned Gemma to steer clear of anyone in the audience department, calling them a bunch of "horny, chain-smoking, *Desperate Housewives* fans." And finally, he let her in on the secret stash of Twinkies.

Clark was going to be a good person to have on her side this summer.

THREE

Gemma stood on the sidewalk outside Dana's apartment. This *was* Dana's apartment, right? Hard to tell, what with *all the people* sitting on the stoop smoking cigarettes and drinking forties. Gemma wasn't sure about private property laws in New York, but this *had* to be illegal.

She got her keys out of her bag and stepped gingerly over a slutty drunk girl. "Excuse me," she muttered.

She unlocked the outer door, stopping dead in her tracks in the foyer. The inner door that was usually deadbolted shut was wide open and über-cool teens packed the hallway in front of her. Gemma hugged her bag to her chest, awkwardly squeezing past rich girls in trendy cocktail dresses discussing Givenchy lip-gloss and the new *it* jeans.

And it wasn't just her imagination—everyone was staring at her.

As far as house parties go, it was pretty tame. No table dancing, no brawls, no cops … yet. Just forty people grinding to Kanye West and Kelly Clarkson, pouring vodka in their Diet Cokes, and being slightly X-rated on the Cox's matching suede sofas. If you played "I spy" you might even spot a starlet or the next Zac Posen, but Gemma was too busy trying to fight her way through the crowds to notice.

"Excuse me!" she yelled in vain. The music was impossibly loud.

She pushed her way into the living room. No sign of Dana or America. At first she thought the house had been taken over by bandits, but she wasn't a complete idiot. It was just hard to believe that Dana would do this to her. Sadly, Gemma's sleep schedule was the last thing on Dana's mind when she'd texted her extended posse about a "small get-together."

Gemma cringed, suddenly realizing that she stood out like a foreign exchange student. What a tragedy. And why was she so nervous? She'd been to parties before. Granted, her scene was more bumper cars than chilled bubbly, but parties are parties.

"Gemma!" Dana screamed from the top of the stairs. She lingered a moment, making sure her pink Nanette Lepore tunic was fully appreciated by all. The dress was gorgeous, but Gemma was a little afraid of what Dana would reveal if she lifted her arms any higher.

No matter, all Dana cared about was the attention. And she got plenty of it. She ran down the steps two at a time and swung her arms around Gemma's neck, planting a pink glossy kiss on her cheek. "You made it!"

"Well, yeah. I *live* here," Gemma replied.

Dana's face fell. "You're mad. Don't be mad, Gemma!" she sang, lacing her fingers between Gemma's and pumping her arms to the music. She shook her hips and puffed out her lips like a Hungry Hungry Hippo. Gemma wanted to stay mad but Dana made that nearly impossible.

"It just sort of happened," Dana shrugged, gesturing toward the masses of drunken delinquents. Ah, *that* explains it. "But I promise it won't last forever. There's a huge party at Bungalow 8 tonight. This is just a teaser." She took a swig of champagne and scanned the room. "Where's America? I've *got* to tell you guys something."

"I don't know," Gemma shrugged. She kept a tight grip on her bag and pressed her body against the wall for safety.

I spy, with my little eye, someone *severely* out of place.

"Who *are* all these people?" she asked, bewildered. "And where's Gabriella?"

"She wasn't invited!" Dana yelled over the Black Eyed Peas. "Lighten up, Gem. She's down in her apartment. As long as there's no drinking she's cool with it, so don't tell her about the case of champagne on ice in my bathtub!"

Dana didn't let herself get bogged down with "right" and "wrong." She guzzled the rest of her champagne and handed the empty flute to Gemma.

"Hold this," Dana ordered. "I'm going to track down America. She's probably reading a fucking book or something."

Gemma watched her trot out of the room, pausing briefly to air kiss a couple snobby blondes. What a schmoozer. Unfortunately Gemma didn't know anyone, so there would be no air kissing in her immediate future. She put Dana's empty glass on a marble table in the foyer and stared at a cluster of girls dancing in front of her. Dana didn't *really* know all these people, did she?

You'd be surprised. Dana had been mingling with the Manhattan elite since she left the womb, thanks to the late Mr. Cox who money managed everyone from The Donald to J. Lo. Add to that a stepmother who socialized with everyone in between and it was only natural that Dana would party with all their offspring. The libations may have changed over the years, but Dana's panache stayed the same. She was an *E! True Hollywood Story* in the making. Still, when word of a house party hits the streets, it's open season.

"You're a friend of Dana's?"

Gemma turned to face the short Latin beauty leaning casually against the wall next to her. It was immediately clear to Gemma that this girl was not to be trifled with. Wild black curls, cheekbones for days, a little black dress that made Gemma blush. Not just blush—Gemma was momentarily speechless.

"Y-yeah," Gemma said, clearing her throat. "I'm Gemma Winters."

"Harper Santos," she purred, caressing a thick diamond choker.

Harper Santos? Puh-lease.

"You look like you could use a drink," Harper observed.

Gemma nodded. Did she have a choice? She scanned the room for a beer bucket or something, a little startled when Harper shoved a full glass of dark, bubbly liquid in her face. Gemma accepted it wearily, sniffing the rim.

"It's a Penny Pincher," Harper told her. She raised her eyebrows, urging Gemma to drink up. "I just made it. They're divine."

"Thanks," Gemma said. She raised the glass to Harper in appreciation and took a large gulp. Interesting. Her mouth felt fiery and sweet at the same time. She took another sip and cocked her head to one side, surveying Dana's living room. Most of these kids were probably Gemma's age, but they all looked so much older.

Not older, Gemma—just wiser.

"So, how do you know Dana?" Gemma asked.

"We both used to summer in Biarritz," Harper replied casually, taking a cigarette out of her Hermès Kelly bag and lighting it with a monogrammed Zippo.

Gemma smiled, feigning interest. Biarritz was in France, right? She twisted her cocktail around in her hand, looking longingly at a group of giggling girls she wished she were talking to instead of Harper. There didn't seem to be anything *evil* about Harper, but Gemma couldn't figure out why the socialite was even talking to her.

"Harper, what an unpleasant surprise," Dana said, re-appearing from the kitchen with America.

At first glance, Gemma thought America looked like an ice cream cone, but if she'd known how much America's elaborately beaded Von Furstenberg dress cost, she might have come up with a more sophisticated analogy.

"Dana! *Great* party, but I've got to motor," Harper said with a venomous smile. She put her cigarette out in an empty glass on the table and laced her bony fingers together. "Jared Leto's having a 'thing' tonight and I promised I'd swing by."

"Totally," Dana nodded, with a poison tongue. "You go 'thing' it up with Jared. Oh, and if the fact that he's filming in Palm Beach detains him, you could always hit Haley Joel Osment's birthday party."

Rrreear.

Ashlee Simpson sang at the top of her lungs while the guests shut up and inched closer. Teens are like drug dogs when it comes to sniffing out a potential catfight. All eyes hung on Dana as she tipped her champagne flute to her lips and knocked back two-thirds of the glass. She linked her arm through Gemma's and glared at Harper. If she weren't so glittery-pink and frosted, Dana would have looked *really* mad.

"Ugh, *that's* why I need bouncers at these things," she yelled, watching Harper storm out of the apartment. "Now come with me to the bathroom!"

She wedged a bottle of champagne under her arm and directed Gemma and America upstairs to the off-limits bathroom in her stepmother's bedroom suite. The soundproofing made it impossible to hear a word of the new Mariah Carey single through the thick marble walls. Dana grabbed a cigarette from her stepmother's secret stash under a pile of washcloths, bouncing from side to side as she lit it. The giddy "I've got a secret" smile plastered across her face meant one thing: love. Or in Dana's case: *lust*. She had a sweet tooth for boys and a habit of jumping from one to the next in what her therapist called "Freudian substitution complex." Therapists *invented* terms after hearing about Dana's life.

"Spit it out!" Gemma laughed. She'd been in a love-free zone since birth, but the signs were universal: shit-eating Mel Tormé grin, glassy eyes, and an overall disinterest in everything else. It was so cute, Gemma wanted to puke with jealousy.

"I'm in love!" Dana swooned, putting her free hand on America's hip. "Dance with me," she ordered.

America grudgingly obliged, stretching out her long arms and cupping her hand around Dana's shoulder blade. They twirled around the bathroom in a mock waltz-cha-cha combo, knocking over everything in sight while they did it. Ah, the picture of elegance. Gemma giggled, a little envious of their tight-knit bond.

"Wait a sec," Gemma said, standing up dizzily and wedging her body between Fred and Ginger. "How can you drag me up here and say you're in love and not *tell* me about it? I'm a girl," Gemma wailed. "I need details: name, hotness on a scale of one to ten, what grade he's in ... It's the guy from the video store, right?"

"Whoa, spazz," Dana said, laughing at Gemma. With her foot, she pulled open a drawer and grabbed another cigarette, ignoring the fact that she'd just put one out. She tried to light it backwards, giggling to herself as she threw the singed filter at a framed photograph of her stepmother taken by Mario Testino. The entire bathroom was a shrine to the woman. Dana pulled yet another cigarette from the pack, concentrating hard to light it properly this time.

Wasted people take *forever* to do things.

"Not that loser," Dana said, rejoining the conversation at her own leisurely pace. "I hit Globe after—"

"But you're not twenty-one," Gemma said innocently.

Forgive Gemma. She grew up in a Little House on the Prairie.

Dana stuck out her relatively new 34Cs and tousled her blonde curls. "Honey, when you look like *this*, it doesn't matter!"

Gemma's cheeks burned. Her 36Cs didn't stand out as much when you added the rest of her chubby body, and living with Kate Moss and Gisele wasn't doing much for her self-esteem, either. Not that Dana had meant it as an insult. She was just too drunk to notice.

"Dana, you are a tactless *fuck*," America purred. Expletives rolled off her tongue like silk on marble.

"I'm kidding, I'm kidding!" Dana cackled, scanning the room for the champagne bottle. "Yes, Gemma. Technically you have to be twenty-one. But there are ways around it. And," she paused, spotting the bottle on the laundry hamper, "I've got a surprise for you. I'm getting you a fake ID!

How hot is that? Now America and I can show you the *real* New York."

Gemma smiled. Well, it was more like her lips curled up in excited fear. Not that clubbing in New York City wouldn't be fun, but with a fake ID? She took a swig of her drink, trying to picture herself at a nightclub. What if she got arrested and her parents had to fly in from Idaho to bail her out?

"I don't know if I should," Gemma hesitated.

"Oh, come on! Don't be such a pussy," Dana whined. She crossed her arms and pretended to scowl at Gemma. It was like having a little sister to manipulate. She didn't want to put Gemma in harm's way or anything—just to the left of harm's way would be fine.

"Listen," Dana said, hoisting herself onto the countertop and kicking her pink sparkly Louboutin slingbacks onto the floor. "Going clubbing isn't code for shooting up heroin. You can just dance if you want. Honestly, the worst that could happen would be that the bouncer guy takes your ID away and tells you to fuck off. No big."

Dana was a master manipulator. If she could convince a headmaster not to expel her after throwing a party in the faculty lounge, then showing Gemma the merits of a fake ID would be cake.

"Really?" Gemma said. She paced the length of the bathroom, shuddering at the sight of her end-of-a-long-day reflection in the mirror, then hopped onto the counter next to Dana. In all honesty, clubbing sounded awesome. "Okay. But I don't want to end up the subject of one of those made-for-TV movies," she added wearily.

"Oh my *god*," Dana said in disgust. She poured the last of the champagne down her throat, tapping the bottle for drops. "You sound like the kids from *7th Heaven*. Don't you want to be a sex-crazed teenager and get a little *Dirrty*, Christina Aguilera style?"

Gemma giggled and nodded reluctantly. The very thought of being rebellious gave her goosebumps.

"Thank god *that's* settled," America sighed, rifling through Mrs. Cox's medicine cabinet. It was like a Betty Ford supply closet. "Now can we get back to Dana's sex life?"

"Well..." Dana grinned and wrapped her arms around her tanned legs. If it weren't for the mega-boobs and Marlboro hanging off her lip she'd look like a five-year-old girl. "He's totally indie-boy sexy. Tall and skinny, brown hair, thrift-store-chic, a musician..."

"Sounds like Bret Lewis all over again," America observed.

Dana sneered at the comparison.

"Who's Bret Lewis?" Gemma asked impatiently.

America grabbed another bottle of Dom and popped it open, careful not to muss her French manicure. She poured champagne into her empty glass and turned to Gemma. "Bret's the drummer for The Likelihood. He was a total fucking moron but Dana got all wet for him. She's a slut for brooding artist types."

"That's not true," Dana whined. She twirled a blonde curl around her pointer finger and continued. "I thought Bret was the bee's knees, but he got all obsessed with me.

He wanted to quit the tour to be with me, blah blah blah. I wonder if that restraining order is still in effect ..."

Restraining order? Sometimes Gemma forgot how different their lives were.

"And don't you act so fucking righteous," Dana added, wagging her finger at America.

"I *might* have slept with the bassist," America admitted, squinting like she'd forgotten to take out the garbage. "But that's *so* not the point," she sighed. She took a few bobby pins out and her hair came cascading down around her heart-shaped face. "We're talking about *your* men issues."

"This guy is *not* Bret. And I don't have *men* issues," Dana huffed. "He's a DJ, which is light years cooler than the drummer of a fuckin' emo band."

"What's his name?" Gemma asked.

Dana opened her mouth to speak and then bit her lip.

"You don't know his *name?*" America shook her head. *So* typical.

"I know it ... *kind of.* It might be Jon, I think. It was really loud in there!" she giggled. It *was* kind of ridiculous that she didn't know the dude's name. "I gave him my number, so if he calls, I'll ask him."

"Slut," America deadpanned.

"Just make sure he's not a psychopath," Gemma said. She hugged her knees into her chest, grazing her chin across her kneecap. "I was totally harassed on the subway this morning, and it freaked me out."

Dana hopped off the counter, picking her shoes up off the floor. "What do you mean?"

Gemma told them about Subway Guy expecting hugs and commiserative pouts, but Dana shrugged and America rolled her eyes. What, so being attacked on the subway *wasn't* a bad thing? She couldn't decide whether to be hurt or humiliated.

"You're not in Kansas anymore," America sang. "He was flirting with you. We're in New York, it happens."

"Really?" Gemma said. She'd never thought about it like that. Her mouth curled slightly. "He *was* kinda cute…"

"Ooh, he vas, vas he? Veeery interestink," Dana mused in her Dr. Ruth voice.

"I had a Subway Guy once…in Paris." America stretched her silky smooth legs out on the rim of the bathtub and looked longingly out the window.

"Did anything ever happen?" Gemma asked, trying not to giggle. America looked like she was about to wax poetic about her first tour in 'Nam.

"No," she sighed. "He smiled and gave me a few seductive French winks. Sometimes I overdo the 'playing hard to get' thing. When I left Paris I never saw him again." She shrugged. "I could at least have made an effort. French guys are great—"

"—*luvahs*?" Dana supplied, über-seductively. She burst out laughing. "Sorry, America. You're so damn serious sometimes. I had to."

America stuck out her tongue, pouting a little, but she didn't look mad. Sophisticated world travelers are bound to have a few sappy sagas. She unlocked the bathroom door and gave Gemma a hand off the counter. They'd been in the bathroom for half an hour, and god knows what kind of shit was going on downstairs.

"You should totally go for that guy if you see him again." Dana had to yell now that they were back in the land of Britney Spears. "You don't have to go down a deserted alley with the guy, but try not to act like a nun, either."

Easy for them to say, Gemma thought, following Dana and America back downstairs. The party was thinning out a bit, but now that she had a buzz she was sort of in the mood to dance. She drained her glass and bobbed her head from side to side, scanning for hotties. How was she going to meet boys and add another chapter to her embarrassingly PG love life if she went to bed at ten o'clock every night?

"Will you come with me to make another drink?" Gemma asked, grabbing Dana's hand.

Dana nodded, leading the way to the extensive wet bar in the living room. "What are you drinking anyway?" Dana asked, grabbing Gemma's empty glass and sniffing it.

"I don't know," Gemma slurred. "Harper gave it to me."

Dana put her hand over her mouth and gasped. "Don't freak out..."

That doesn't sound good.

"...but I think Harper gave you a Penny Pincher."

"Yeah?" Gemma said. *And the problem with that is...*

"She does that. It's her 'thing,'" Dana said, making air quotes disdainfully. "She gets a bunch of people to spit some of their drink into a glass and then she gives it to the new kid. It's called a 'Penny Pincher' because you save money by spitting leftover sips into one big, skankdified concoction. I'm *so* sorry Gemma."

Not as sorry as Gemma was. Ten seconds later she was back in the bathroom praying to the porcelain god. Fun party.

FOUR

Mikayla Ostroff rolled her eyes as Gemma stumbled into work ten minutes late on Tuesday. The marathon pukefest had sort of thrown her off schedule. She ran in, completely out of breath, her spiky Manolos nearly giving way beneath her as she screeched to a halt. The grumpiest—not to mention burliest—of the three *Back Talk* production assistants was standing in the middle of the room tapping her loafer-clad foot impatiently. Didn't she have anything better to do?

"You're *finally* here," Mikayla scolded, folding her muscular arms across her chest. She had this Mia Hamm thing going on that made Gemma skittish.

"H-hi," Gemma replied meekly.

A pair of small, sassy brunettes fanned out from behind Mikayla like sidekicks in a kung fu flick. Standing there with matching self-important smirks, they looked suspiciously like the Olsen twins, only Hispanic and better fed.

"Meet Maria and Anita Cruz," Mikayla said, nodding over her shoulder at the twins.

"*I'm* Maria," one of them said, stepping out from behind Mikayla. She folded her arms over her white C&C top.

Gemma waved self-consciously, pressing her elbows tightly to her sides. It would be easy to tell them apart, what with Maria actually having style and everything. Maybe Gemma could only afford Gap, but at least she didn't wear the Jessica Simpson Dessert perfume that was unmistakably wafting from Anita's pink mesh T-shirt.

"Timothy's on a field shoot with quintuplet strippers from Jersey," Mikayla explained. "He needs me to help Val type up the script before the staff meeting so you're on copy machine duty. The twins are already working," she added, rubbing in Gemma's tardiness. "Maria, you're in charge. Fill Gemma in, okay?"

She ran out of the room like her buns of steel were on fire, leaving Gemma with a tepid Maria and a yet-to-be-branded Anita.

"Take this stack," Maria ordered. She pulled her wavy brown hair around the side of her neck and thrust a stack of papers in Gemma's face. "Make twelve collated copies and separate them into those purple folders."

And hello to you, too.

Maria's forbidding tone sent a chill down Gemma's spine. The girls were both pretty enough with similar watery brown eyes, tropical tans, and long layered hair, but there was something *off* about Maria. A certain Sarah Michelle Gellar in *Cruel Intentions* quality—though hopefully Maria wasn't hot for her own sister.

"I've never met twins before," Gemma said, attempting small talk. It was futile, but she couldn't help trying. She rifled through a stack of articles and slid them into the copier. "Do people confuse you all the time?"

"No," Maria snapped. "Anita's not as pretty as me. Couldn't you tell?"

Ouch.

"As *if!*" Anita giggled, taking Maria's insult for a game. "*I'm* the prettier one!"

"Well, it's nice to meet you guys," Gemma said, not about to get in the middle of a beauty competition.

She subtly felt the armpit of her gray cotton shirt for sweat stains. After sprinting from the subway to the office she was hot and sticky. "Are you interns, too?" she asked.

"For now," Maria yawned, separating stacks of original and photocopied pre-interviews. "I'm sure you've heard of our father, Robert Cruz. I don't think we'll be interns for long." She smiled deliberately.

"Robert Cruz?" Gemma repeated in awe. The man was, like, Mr. Television. He probably had an entire roomful of Emmy awards.

"Come here," Anita said sweetly, motioning to her workstation on the floor. "I didn't want to be an intern. *I* wanted to go on a cruise this summer." She paused for *oohs* and *ahhs* as Gemma perched on the coffee-stained carpet. "But Daddy was all, 'No. Get a job.' So, like, here we are!"

Like, wow. A real live Valley Girl.

"We're starting our first semester at Yale this fall," she added. "It's super prestigious."

"Yeah, I've heard of Yale," Gemma said flatly. *Yale* had accepted these idiots? Nice to see that nepotism was alive and well.

"I got a fifteen hundred on my SATs. Maria's just tagging along!"

"No, *I* got the fifteen hundred," Maria growled, appearing next to them. Her Jimmy Choo boot nearly crushed Gemma's finger. "You slept your way into Yale, remember?"

Diz*zamn*. Maria had quite the poison tongue. And weren't twins supposed to have the same IQ? Maybe Anita had been dropped on her head as a baby.

"Yo, girlies!" Melissa chirped, popping her head into Hell. She brought the smell of a flower shop with her. "Staff meeting in the conference room."

Gemma's heart raced. She heard the pitter-patter of KMers shuffling into the conference room and panicked. The idea of a staff meeting made her want to vomit. *As long as they don't formally introduce me as the doe-eyed intern from Idaho, I'll be fine.* She stood up wearily, following Anita out of the room.

"Wait, Gemma," Maria hollered. "Don't forget your purse."

Gemma smiled quizzically and accepted her crappy canvas bag. Why would she need *that* in the staff meeting? The three of them walked into the conference room and searched around for seats. The mile-long boardroom table was already full, and Gemma felt like a lost puppy until she spotted Clark Dobbs sitting in a chair against the wall.

"Hey!" Gemma said, settling into the seat next to him. She eyed the *Back Talk with Kate Morgan* notepad in his lap and gulped. No one had given *her* any official stationery. Sob. It was a totally fifth-grade response, but she was jealous. Not to mention intimidated. Clark's starched lilac shirt and shiny alligator loafers looked *muy expensivo.*

"So, what's the deal with this staff meeting?"

"They're every Tuesday," Clark yawned, twirling his staff ID badge around on his palm. "It's no big. Some brainiac makes a dumb joke about a newspaper headline. Penelope goes over show ratings and upcoming shows. Sometimes we even talk about show budgets—ten thousand bucks, fifty thousand... Booor-ing."

Gemma unclenched her shoulders a little. Dumb jokes and ratings sounded doable. She crossed her legs and tugged at her short black Delia's skirt, nearly fainting as Nick Daltrey sauntered past. God, he was practically edible. How could one guy look *so* good in simple jeans and an untucked button-down shirt and tie? Gemma smiled. *Yum.* She may have been the innocent girl next door, but cable TV gave her a wild imagination.

"Good morning, people."

A hush fell over the crowd as a more-than-slightly intimidating six-foot-one redhead in a sleek white Prada suit strut briskly into the conference room. She put her briefcase and handbag down, taking a quick sip of a Starbucks Venti something. It was Penelope O'Shea, the executive producer and chief decision maker of all things *Back Talk*. Gemma once read an article about her in *Marie Claire* called "The Toughest Broad in TV"—the title seemed fitting.

"Let's get this out of the way. I have a busy day and I hope you all do, too." Ms. O'Shea's melodic Irish accent was pretty, but everything else about her screamed Drill Sergeant. "Good work on last week's shows, people," she said, rifling through her gold-sequined bag. She pulled out a *Back Talk* memo pad and scanned the room before continuing. "Ratings went through the roof for 'Get Your Sex Drive in Gear.' Nice job, Deniece. We beat *Oprah* in our Florida and New York markets and did a 7.6 average for the week."

Gemma smiled, trying to hide her confusion. Maybe she would have been ooohing and aaahing along with everyone else if she'd known that 7.6 represented nearly ten million household viewers. On its own it sounded more like a pathetic roomful of stay-at-home moms.

"James, your team is down this week, but you've got the go-ahead for teen prostitution. Of course, there are a few stipulations, but we all know what *that* means," Ms. O'Shea joked knowingly.

Of course, Gemma pretended.

Sleazy James made a "whoop, whoop" noise accompanied by a manly wrist pump. Gemma's lips curled in disgust.

What a cretin. James probably spent high school terrorizing defenseless nerds and now he made six figures. Not exactly payback.

"Next," said the Irish beauty, tapping her notepad with a fountain pen.

Gemma studied her as she spoke, wondering if the small lines around her eyes and mouth meant she was, like, forty or if she just looked that old.

"Kate plugged 'Moms on Ecstasy' and 'Operation: Teen Sex Change' on *Entertainment Tonight* so we've got to knock those shows out of the—"

Dinenene-dinenene-dineneneneee...

Everyone jumped as the generic Nokia tune blasted through the room. Gemma cringed. Some poor schmuck had forgotten to turn off his cell phone before the meeting. She'd left hers at home, thank god.

Dinenene-dinenene-dineneneneee...

"God damn it!" Ms. O'Shea screamed, pounding a jeweled fist on the table. "Whoever's that is, just turn it off!"

Dinenene-dinenene-dineneneneee...

Gemma squirmed in her seat, looking from side to side. Shouldn't the thing have gone to voicemail by now? It had been ringing for*ever*. At the head of the table, Ms. O'Shea's creamy white face turned a deep shade of rage-driven red. Gemma winced, suddenly wondering if people ever *actually* exploded.

Dinenene-dinenene-dineneneneee...

Damn! Like the Nokia ringtone wasn't obnoxious enough, now it had to ruin a staff meeting? The tension in the conference room was almost unbearable. One by one, staffers reached in their pockets and opened their purses to double check, but the ringing persisted.

Dinenene-dinenene-dinenenenee...

"Uh, Gemma?" Clark whispered.

"Yeah," Gemma whispered back, her face feeling hotter and hotter.

"I think your phone's ringing."

Nauseous and pale, Gemma reached for her bag with trembling hands. Slowly, eyes shot across the room toward her, none more penetrating than Penelope O'Shea's. Gemma groped around in her bag, first pulling out a tampon, then a pack of Trident, and finally, inexplicably, a black Nokia cell phone.

Where had *that* come from?

"Well?" the Irish drill sergeant snarled. "Turn the damn thing off!"

Gemma's clammy hands gripped the phone, quickly pressing END and every other button. Sheepishly jamming the mystery phone back into her bag, she sunk as low as possible in her chair. This was *beyond* humiliating.

Now that the ringing had stopped, you could hear a pin drop.

"I am so, so, *so*—"

"Let's just get on with it," Ms. O'Shea said tersely. "Is there anything else?"

Silence. The painfully awkward kind.

"Are we having pitch meetings today, Penelope?"

Gemma raised her head, silently praising the older woman in an orange Lilly Pulitzer sweater for breaking the silence. Orange was all wrong on her but at least *she* hadn't ruined the staff meeting. Gemma focused on orange-sweater-lady—Nina maybe?—and bit her lip to keep from crying.

Ms. O'Shea nodded, her eye lingering on Gemma for another five seconds. "Yes," she finally answered. "At least five ideas from each production team. And no more goddamn war stories. Kate's not a bloody Marine and viewers are tuning out by segment two. They want to see her sparkle," she enthused with bulging green eyes. She quickly looked down at her shiny Chanel watch and sighed. "Thanks to the *interruption* I'm late for a meeting."

As if on cue, everyone turned to get one last look at The Culprit. Ms. O'Shea mumbled something then whipped her Blackberry out of her bag. "Everyone back to work." She grabbed her things and sprinted out of the conference room, her assistant at her heels. Apparently the meeting was adjourned.

With a sigh of relief, Gemma scurried out as fast as her little Manolos would let her and ran to the bathroom. If she stayed in the conference room, someone might reprimand her for her inappropriate cell phone use. Like she didn't already know. The bathroom was empty and she picked the farthest stall to lock herself in, collapsing onto the toilet seat. It smelled like poo and stale cigarettes, but she didn't want to leave. Her lower lip quivered as she rehashed the nightmare. Out of all her fatalistic work scenarios, she'd never pictured *this*. It was too confusing. Had a mugger *given* her a phone instead of stealing one from her?

The bathroom door swung open and a pair of heels clicked over to the bathroom sink. Gemma pawed at the toilet paper, quickly drying her tears, and flushed the toilet. As much as she wanted to, she couldn't hide in the little girls' room all day. She took a few deep breaths, pushing the stall door open.

"Hey, you," Maria said with a sympathetic frown. "You okay?"

Of course not, but Gemma didn't want to look like a baby. "Yeah, thanks." She bent over the sink and splashed some cold water on her face. The water smelled funny but it felt good, so she splashed herself again and looked up at her reflection in the mirror. Maria was holding out a wad of paper towels for her.

"Thanks, Maria. I really appreciate it." Gemma suddenly felt bad for being so quick to judge. "Don't tell anyone I cried, okay?"

Maria shook her head and promised, "No worries. You're secret's safe with me." She winked at Gemma and turned toward the door. "Oh, one more thing?"

Gemma looked up eagerly from her paper towel and nodded.

"Can I just grab my cell phone out of your bag?"

Waiting a millisecond to relish Gemma's gaping, dumbfounded speechlessness, Maria trotted back over and dug around in the bag, pulling out the evil Nokia.

"Thanks, sweetie!" She slipped the phone into the back pocket of her Sevens and skipped out of the bathroom.

FIVE

The nickname "Nokia Girl" only lasted a day, thank *god*. By the time Thursday rolled around everyone was done snickering and back to treating Gemma like any old bottom-of-the-barrel intern. And she'd learned a valuable lesson: people suck.

"Hey, doll!"

It was Deniece, the busty blonde producer with the crazy Long Island accent. "I was just looking for one of you guys. Do me a plus?" she said, pulling a receipt and a wad of cash out of her wallet. "I've got a prescription down at Duane Reade on Fifty-Third. Run and grab it for me?" She didn't even wait for a response before whining, "Thanks, hon," and taking off down the hallway.

Gemma huffed indignantly. There was nobody around to hear it, but she felt Deniece's condescension deserved an audible notation. She counted the money, put it and the receipt in her pocket, and took the elevator down to the ground floor. It was too hot to be crammed up in an office anyway—especially now that she was on perma-lookout for the Sabotage Twins.

There were a few KMers smoking outside, but Gemma rushed past them. She *could* have stopped to say hi, but then what? What comes after hi? (a) Gemma didn't smoke, and (b) *she* was the butt of the only gossip she knew. Sad but true. She turned the corner onto Broadway and froze. Crowded was a bold understatement. Finally, she did a quick bob-and-weave combo, fighting her way down Broadway like it was a Tae Bo video.

Duane Reade eventually appeared before her like an oasis and she ran in, grateful for the AC. Gemma handed Deniece's prescription to the Indian dude behind the counter and took a seat on the grungy plastic chair provided. She slouched a little and let her eyes drift shut. It was the perfect opportunity to fantasize about the graphics intern … *It's a hot, steamy afternoon. Gemma and Nick get stuck in the elevator. In a passionate rage, Nick tears Gemma's clothes off …*

Somebody's been reading Harlequin.

A half hour later, Gemma grabbed the pills, fighting the temptation to read the label. What a good girl. She wandered outside, diving back into her Nick fantasies … *Soaked and cold from an unexpected rainstorm, Nick appears with an*

umbrella. They hide out in a café for hours, sipping hot choco-
late and discussing art and poetry…

"Hey," a loud, slurring voice boomed, crushing Gemma's daydream. She clutched her bag tightly to her chest, looking directly into the face of a dirty homeless man. He smelled like pee, and the raggedy Texas A&M sweatshirt he had on was covered in… something. Gemma had never come face to face with a homeless person before.

You don't say.

"Ss'a pretty day, huh? Can a nice girl like you shpare shome change?"

Gemma's heart thudded furiously. All around her people breezed past, not a single one of them stopping to help her. She dodged to the right and faked to the left, but the home-less guy's needy face and thick arms blocked both attempts. What was she supposed to do? If she opened her wallet to get some change the guy might steal the entire thing.

"I don't have anything, sorry," Gemma sputtered. She looked down at her Manolos and a pang of guilt flooded her body.

"Come on, honey," he purred, burping nasty god-knows-what in Gemma's face.

She spun around so fast that she almost fell flat on her face, but the homeless guy reached out to steady her.

"Thanks." She smiled at his kindness, suddenly feeling like a total hypocrite. With a frantic gesture she wriggled free from his grasp and stumbled backwards. She let the sea of New Yorkers swallow her up and carry her away, vaguely hearing the guy yell "Bitch!" as she went.

SIX

"Here you go, Chanel Jones," Dana said, pulling a laminated card out of her white, quilted Marc Jacobs bag like it was Willy Wonka's golden ticket. She tugged at her maroon tube top and propped up on one elbow, eagerly awaiting Gemma's response.

"Chanel?" Gemma sneered, snatching the brand-new fake ID away from Dana. "Did you steal it from a *porn* star?" She scratched at the photo with her stubby fingernails, marveling at its authenticity. Waiting an entire week for the thing had been excruciating, and now that it was in her hands she was practically orgasmic—even if her name *was* Chanel.

"Beggars can't be choosers, Chanel!" Dana giggled.

She and Gemma were both insanely giddy. You would be too if you were spending Friday night partying like a rock star at *the* new club, Slip. Slip was the brainchild of club owner extraordinaire Vincent Argos, and anybody who's anybody would be at the opening. The whole idea had Gemma bordering on cardiac arrest, but she tried to reserve all panic attacks for the solitude of her bedroom. Dana, on the other hand, would need a tranq gun to keep her away. She was on a permanent quest to hit every VIP room in Manhattan, whereas America, moderately less dazzled, was just along for the ride.

"Your name is the least of your worries," America said, filing her nails on the leopard print chaise in Dana's room. The way her long, lean, Juicy-clad body molded its contours, you'd think she was in the middle of a *Vogue* cover shoot.

"What do you mean?" Gemma asked, scrutinizing the card in the glow of an antique lamp beside Dana's bed. Her hair looked good in the photograph and there were no visible zits or double chins; the fake address looked credible; there was even a hologram. Gemma couldn't tell what th—

"Dana!" Gemma blushed with embarrassment, nearly bursting into tears. "It says I'm twenty-seven!"

A temper tantrum should disprove *that* quick enough.

"I know," Dana groaned. She pulled a Parliament Menthol out of her bedside drawer and padded over to her window to light it. Gemma's reaction was to be expected. "But I swear it'll work. We just have to … alter you a little."

"Whoa, what do you mean *alter*?"

"Hmm," America said. In a smooth, catlike motion, she arose from the chaise and sauntered over to Gemma. She pulled the zipper of her charcoal gray Juicy sweatshirt up and down, peering down her nose at the girl from the sticks.

Gemma rolled her shoulders back and lifted her chin up and to the side. This felt very *America's Next Top Model*. More like America's latest science experiment. But honestly, millionheiresses do the best makeovers.

"I think we can do this," America decided, taking a chunk of Gemma's long brown hair and teasing it into a bouffant. She unclipped the Gucci barrette from her own brown tresses, temporarily securing her creation. "That works. We'll put you in something low cut, and do smoky Ashlee Simpson eyes."

"You'll look hot!" Dana whooped. She flicked her cigarette out the window and began circling her room like a hawk, scooping up jewelry and accessories to add to the cause.

Great, Gemma thought. Looking like Ashlee Simpson was hardly incentive, but if she didn't do it she was afraid they'd go to Slip without her.

America nipped across the hall to her room and came back holding a black silk, kimono-style Rebecca Taylor top with a seriously plunging neckline. Turning to face the wall for privacy, Gemma tossed her T-shirt on the floor and pulled the blouse over her head. It took a little more force than she would have liked.

"You want me to wear *this*?" Gemma gasped, blushing at the sight of her heaving bosom reflected in the full-length mirror. She'd feel a lot better once she saw the half-naked tramps at Slip.

"Are you sure, America?" she asked. "You're much thinner than me. What if I rip it?"

"You won't," America swore, though her tone was less than convincing. "Besides," she added, peeling off her Tsubi skinny jeans and holding a colorful Missoni skirt up to her waist. "I already wore it to that Whitney benefit. You'll be rescuing it from Salvation Army." She tossed the skirt on Dana's bed and grabbed a black dress in exchange. It was Lanvin, but only a handful of label snobs would have noticed. "You don't mind my hand-me-downs, right? I hate to repeat an outfit and you make me feel like a Good Samaritan."

Gemma smiled awkwardly. They lived on completely different planets.

"Dana, what do you think of this top?" Gemma asked. "Is it too boobalicious?"

"You look hot," Dana replied. She wasn't really paying attention—too busy texting half the world on her bedazzled Sidekick—but it was a pointless question anyway. Asking Dana if something was too boobalicious was like asking Imelda Marcos if you could own too many shoes.

"Who wants champagne?" Dana asked, jumping off the bed and pulling a chilled bottle of Moët out of a sterling silver ice bucket on the dresser. It was after seven and *way* past cocktail hour. Tearing away the metal foil, she popped the cork like a pro, giggling as it sailed across her bedroom like a bullet. She took a quick sip from the bottle and sighed with appreciation.

She filled two glasses to the brim, handing them to her friends, and kept the rest of the bottle for herself.

"Cheers, biatches!" she said, tilting the bottle to her mouth. "Refills?"

America shook her head.

"In a minute," Gemma responded. Was it a race? She twirled her glass around in her hand and watched Dana chug champagne by the window. Not to be all "*7th Heaven*" or whatever, but her bad girl style was a little intense. Three Bud Lights on a Saturday night was all the excitement Gemma was used to.

"Keep drinking and go find yourself some sexy jeans," Dana ordered. She pulled her top off over her head, revealing bare breasts, and opened the door to her walk-in closet. Gemma quickly looked away, but modesty wasn't an issue for Dana. Boarding school has that effect.

"Oh, what about shoes for you?" Dana added. "My feet are frickin' huge and you're only an eight, right?"

"She could try those silver Gucci sandals I found at Bergdorf," America said to Dana, casually cradling her champagne glass in her hand. She took a dainty sip, tilting her head to look at Gemma through the mirror. "They'd work with that top," she decided.

"Wow, thanks," Gemma said, gratefully appreciative as usual. Of course she was dying to wear designer shoes, but she felt like their charity case. Well, she *was*.

She took a small sip of champagne. She *could* stand up for herself and tell them she didn't appreciate being treated like a human Barbie doll...but this was Gucci at stake, so she kept her mouth shut.

"I'll grab the shoes, you grab the jeans," America said, humming something Top 40ish as she skipped out of the room. She really *did* seem to enjoy sharing her stuff. But Gemma felt bad never having anything to repay her with. *I could bake her some cookies*, she mused.

Yeah, or give her a kidney.

"Sexy jeans, sexy jeans" Gemma sighed to herself, grabbing her T-shirt off Dana's floor. She took the last sip of her champagne, enjoying the warm fuzzies, and dragged her feet down the hall to her room. Did she even *own* sexy jeans? With four pairs to choose from, the search wouldn't be long. Suddenly a wave of nausea swelled in her stomach. *Can I really pull this off?* The sex-kitten top made her feel like a clown, and if her parents knew what she was up to, they would freak.

BACK TALK

The cab pulled up outside Slip and Gemma's confidence plummeted from a four to a one. She clenched the door handle with a clammy palm, too afraid to just open the thing and get out. It *was* intimidating, no question. And this Argos guy had pulled out all the stops: waterfalls streaming down shiny granite walls, bamboo-relief gold doors, glitterati out in droves. It was yummy trendy goodness way beyond Gemma's comprehension, and Japanese design is *so* in right now.

Dana's Sidekick rang for the fifth time in twenty minutes and she giggled looking at the caller ID. "Move it or lose it," she bellowed, leaning over Gemma's paralyzed body to open the door. "Hey there, stranger," she purred in a 1-900-number voice.

Gemma got out of the cab, awkwardly covering her cleavage with her handbag. She wasn't much for the "grand entrance." America, on the other hand, looked like Audrey Hepburn as she emerged from the dingy taxi. Heads turned in admiration and awe as she paused to stroke her swanlike neck before gliding onto the sidewalk.

Who can compete with that?

"Wrap it up, Dana," America snapped, tapping her watch.

"Aren't you nervous?" Gemma asked.

America pulled a Nars lipstick out of her clutch and pressed it to her full lips for a touch-up. The girl ached elegance.

"Clubbing's overrated." She shrugged as if she were talking about going to the dentist. "The auction at Christie's next week is more my scene."

Gemma nodded for no reason—like *she'd* ever been to an auction house. She reached into her own bag for some lip-gloss, failing pathetically to emulate America. Why did she feel like a self-help book? Probably because she was silently chanting, *I'm smart, I'm cute, and I'm funny!* She tugged at her low-cut top, waiting for America to say something, *anything* she could relate to.

"I love Dana to death, so I let her drag me out from time to time. And it'll be fun to walk you through it, but I'm over the wild-n-crazy teenager thing," she said dully. Her eye drifted down to the oval sapphire ring on her right ring finger. She'd been given it on her sweet sixteen along with a diamond tennis bracelet and an apologetic note from her parents for missing the event. It didn't take a genius to see that America was sick to death of "the good life."

"The Boston aristocracy—a.k.a. 'my people'—doesn't *do* wild-n-crazy." As if reading Gemma's mind, she added, "If you think *I'm* stuck up you should meet my parents."

"I don't think you're stuck up," Gemma lied. "Your family sounds..."

"You have no idea," America replied with ice-cold contempt. "Fuck this," she sighed, kicking Dana with her Prada pump. She grabbed Gemma's arm, and walked briskly toward Slip's bamboo doors.

"So*rrry*," Dana whined, shutting her Sidekick and running to catch up.

"Dana, give me a cigarette," Gemma said as they neared the gold velvet ropes.

"No way!" Dana chuckled, waving at Julia Stiles and some greasy hanger-on. "I know why you're asking, but believe me, one puff and you'll start gagging and look even younger than you think you do."

Gemma sighed. *How else am I supposed to relax?* The champagne helped but it was wearing off. She took a few yogic breaths and stepped forward when the super-tall brunette in front of her did. More liquid encouragement would do the trick, but it's not like she carried a flask.

Gemma faced Slip's ginormo bouncer and pulled her ID out of her purse. He recognized Dana instantly and let her pass through the ropes without hesitation. Then America flashed her ID and breezed through, but he held his palm up, blocking Gemma.

"Hold on, kid," said the three-hundred-pound bald guy.

He put his hand on Gemma's shoulder, scrutinizing the fake license. Her palms dripped with sweat and her heart thumped like cheesy techno. She tried to smile casually, but it translated to something more along the lines of constipation.

I'm going to die, she panicked. *I'll have to take the subway home all by myself at midnight on a Friday night, and I'll die.*

Everyone's gotta have a plan B.

She glanced across the rope frantically. Surely Dana didn't *mean* to abandon her, hanging all over some R. Kelly wannabe like he was a McDonald's playland. Gemma tucked a loose strand of hair behind her ear and tried to act nonchalant. The bouncer dude wasn't buying it. He started to shake his head, handing the two-hundred-dollar useless piece of shit back to her.

"Wait," Gemma begged, backing away from her fake ID. The fear of going home by herself had somehow driven her to grow a pair. She scanned the crowd desperately, suddenly spotting—in the form of a graphics intern—her savior.

"Nick!" Gemma shouted.

Nick Daltrey turned toward her voice and walked closer. "Hey Ge—"

"It's me, *Chanel*, remember?" Gemma quickly interjected, her eyes the size of golf balls.

Nick chuckled. "Right. *Chanel*." He leaned over and gave Gemma a quick kiss on the cheek. "Hey Charlie, Chanel's with me."

"Thanks," Gemma whispered, momentarily stunned by Nick's velvety lips and spicy cologne.

Big, bald, three-hundred-pound Charlie handed Gemma her ID and unhooked the gold velvet rope. Nick was like her mega-hot fairy godmother.

"Thank you so, *so* much," she gushed.

Nick gave her a sexy half smile. "No problem. New fake ID?"

"Nick, is it?" Dana interrupted. Funny how she managed to reappear *after* a cute guy entered the picture. "I'm Dana and this is America. Thanks for getting our girl past Charlie. I'm going to crucify the guy who made her ID."

"It's cool. The owner's a friend of the family," Nick boasted.

"*You* know Vincent Argos?" Dana exclaimed. "You'll have to introduce me."

"He'd love that," Nick said with a nasty grin. "I'm meeting some friends inside. You ladies want to join us for a cocktail?"

Gemma nodded, practically fainting as Nick took her hand and led her inside.

"Holy shit!" she gasped once she'd crossed Slip's threshold. Her eyes darted from side to side, committing every single detail to memory. Even with pictures to prove it, her friends back home would *never* believe the bright gold walls melting into black satin banquettes, or the black lacquered, Swarovski-studded tables that slowly revolved like wind-up toys. Gemma thought she was in glittery gold-and-black heaven.

Actually, the place looked more like Liberace threw up all over a dojo.

Mary J. Blige blared at an ungodly decibel from a DJ booth high above the crowd and hundreds of beautiful people danced to the beat. The cliques of schmoozing socialites sipping apple martinis and highballs were impenetrable, but Gemma didn't care. She was following the hottest guy in the room to a reserved banquette in the corner—although she *did* almost pee in her pants when they passed Bow Wow talking to Lindsay Lohan.

"This place is amazing," she yelled to America, whose response was a half-assed nod. They reached the banquette, where they were greeted by a gaggle of NYU frat boys, and scootched in around the table. It was cramped and loud as hell, but nobody was complaining. Dana always enjoyed being sandwiched between burly football players and America didn't seem to mind much, either. Gemma was just happy to be nestled in next to Nick, who, by the way, was fondly ogling her busty bustline. For the first time all night she stopped tugging self-consciously at the shirt and just enjoyed her apparent sex appeal.

"You don't say," America replied indifferently to the reptilian superjock in chinos and a Lacoste polo. The football jocks and their you-had-to-be-there NYU anecdotes were swiftly losing appeal. "Can we get the *hell* out of here?" she whispered to Dana.

"Hold on a sec." Dana nodded toward Gemma and Nick. "It's like watching a mating ritual on the Discovery Channel," she whispered, giggling at sloppy, horny Gemma. They were all pretty toasted from the two pre-bought bottles of Ketel One swiveling around the table every two minutes, but Gemma had never mixed her own drinks before. After a few *very* screwy screwdrivers she was a giggly cuddle-bunny with no inhibitions.

"It's too bad I don't see you more at work," Gemma whispered, nuzzling her face in Nick's neck. She closed her eyes, enjoying the feeling of his hand on her thigh. *Where had all this confidence come from?* Gemma wondered.

It's called vodka.

"Gemma," America yelled from across the table. "Can I talk to you for a minute?"

Gemma shook her head firmly and turned back for more of Nick's undivided attention. "You have such gorgeous eyes," she told him, caressing his cheek. She let her hand drift down his face and onto his chest, drawing figure eights down the length of his torso with her index finger.

"Oh yeah?" Nick said. He grabbed her hand before it reached his groin and laced her fingers between his.

Gemma had pretty much given him the go-ahead, so he leaned in and kissed her neck. His soft lips made Gemma giggle. She'd always wondered how it would feel to have a guy kiss her neck. It felt sexy. Nick licked his lips and turned Gemma's face toward his.

"So, Nick," Dana interrupted from two seats over. "You're in graphics?"

Nick nodded, dropping Gemma's hand and grabbing his beer.

"And you know Argos," she mused. "Hey, can I bum a smoke?" She leaned closer and grazed her fingertips along Nick's knuckles.

Gemma cleared her throat deliberately, wondering if all of a sudden she'd gone invisible. She knocked back the dregs of her screwdriver and glared at Dana.

"Would you excuse us for a minute?" she yelled to Nick. Her voice was slurred but her anger was crystal clear.

She stood up, waiting a moment for her double vision to become one. Poor thing. She didn't even know why the room was spinning. Nick put his hand on her back to steady her, but she brushed it away, suddenly feeling like his used car.

"Come on, honey," Dana said, taking Gemma's arm.

Gemma wanted to pull away, but not as much as she *didn't* want to fall over, so she gave up and let Dana and America lead her through hordes of spastic crunk dancers to the bathroom.

"*Well?*" Gemma exploded, giving Dana the opportunity to explain.

"I'm trying to save you from humiliating yourself," Dana yelled. "If it wasn't for me, Nick would have you bent over the table by now!"

America snickered and Gemma teetered back, finally stumbling onto a plush gold sofa.

"It's true," America said. Her aristocratic tone was always so demoralizing. "I tried to stop you, but you completely disregarded me." She spotted the bathroom attendant and bought a bottle of FIJI water, handing it to Gemma.

"Well, you didn't have to be so slutty about it, Dana," Gemma grumbled, fumbling with the bottle cap. "Was I really embarrassing myself?"

"Yes," America said bluntly. She rarely softened the blow. She perched on the arm of the sofa, her short black Stella McCartney dress shimmying up around her ass. "Here," she said, unscrewing the bottle cap and handing it back to Gemma. "You're not much of a drinker, are you?"

Gemma shook her head, gulping the water down.

"Let me give you some advice: match every cocktail with at least one glass of water. And you're not allowed to mix your own drinks anymore." America gently rubbed Gemma's back, encouraging slow, peaceful deep breaths.

Gemma looked over her shoulder, making sure it was actually America behind her. Hard to believe, but America *could* be maternal. She just hadn't learned it from her mother.

"The room's still spinning," Gemma complained, trying to hold her head still. She was drunk, tired, nauseous, and completely mortified. She looked up and glowered at two snickering onlookers.

"Thanks for stopping me from … whatever I was about to do," she whispered. "And you swear you weren't trying to steal Nick?"

"No way!" Dana gasped, offended beyond belief.

"No way?" America sneered. "Let's not kid ourselves."

Dana dropped her Dior lip stain in the marble sink, appalled at America's accusation. She was an Oscar-worthy liar, but America had a point. Dana wet a cool washcloth and brought it over to Gemma. If she was going to fess up, she needed to set the mood. "Here sweetie, you look a little peaked. This'll cool you down." Then she stretched out on the sofa, resting her blonde curly head on Gemma's lap. "Okay. I was being *un poco* flirty, but only because (a) I wanted to stop you from doing something you'd regret, and (b) Nick *has* to introduce me to Argos."

"Right, Vincent Argos," Gemma remembered. "Did I ruin your chances?"

"Don't worry about me, honey. I got moves you neva' *seen!*" Dana purred, raising her eyebrows. She stood up, grabbing Gemma's arms and pulling her to her feet. "Will you ix-nay on the ewdrivers-scray?"

"Don't worry," Gemma promised. "I'm so embarrassed. I'm never drinking again."

Raise your hand if you've said *that* before.

"Oh god, what am I going to do about Nick?" Gemma moaned. "I have to *work* with him."

"He's tanked, too. Just write it off. But," Dana added, smiling lecherously as she stood up. "I definitely advise tapping that ass when you're sober."

"God, Dana. You need to be muzzled," America sighed, paying the attendant for two more bottles of water.

"You know you love me!" Dana sang, dirty dancing with America just to embarrass her. "Now, drink that nonalcoholic sludge and let's get the hell out of here. I didn't wear this dress so I could sit in the bathroom with you bitches all night."

Gemma giggled and turned to check out her reflection before they left. Her hair was a little messy but it passed for heroin-chic, and surprisingly, her smoky Ashlee Simpson eyes were still intact.

The girls strutted out of the bathroom and made a beeline for the dance floor. Dana quickly separated from them, running over to a group of B-listers she recognized. Dancing was a bit of a chore for Gemma, but it sort of sobered her up. She shook her hips to cheesy Beyoncé remixes, relieved that she and America could dance instead of talk.

Plus, this beat the hell out of sitting at Nick's table. How embarrassing. She did her best to dance away the horror of what a slut she'd been, but that was nearly impossible.

BACK TALK

The girls stumbled up Dana's front stoop at four a.m. like they were climbing Mt. Everest. Four hours of cardio booty shakin' will do that to a person.

"Shit!" America shrieked, tripping on the steps and top-pling over. Apparently *someone* didn't take her own water-to-alcohol ratio advice.

Gemma burst out laughing. She bent down to help America up, first pausing to enjoy the moment. America splayed out on the steps with her perky butt in the air was *priceless*.

"Sshhh!" Dana stage whispered as they barreled through the outer door and into the vestibule. She stared at her jumbo keychain and selected the appropriate key for the inner door.

Gemma snorted with laughter, then America laughed at her for snorting. Gemma had to put her hand on America's shoulder to keep from falling over. Drinking made America a *lot* more fun. For a millisecond Gemma considered replacing America's morning java with Irish coffee.

"The door won't open," Dana observed a little *too* casually. She took a step back and furrowed her brow. The wooden door must have weighed eighty pounds, but there was nothing complicated about the deadbolt. It *should* have opened.

Uh-oh, girls...

"Maybe your hundredth tequila shot killed your hand-eye coordination." America giggled. "Gimme," she snapped, grabbing the keys from Dana.

"What's your prob, Bob," Dana slurred, lighting her last menthol and tossing the empty pack over her head.

"I can't get it open, either," America huffed. "I just tried the key, like, five times."

Five … four … three … two … Gemma started to panic. She looked around the small foyer they were standing in, wondering if the walls were *actually* closing in on her. If she stopped to think about it rationally for two seconds she would have realized that they had a million options—*hello*, Gabriella was right downstairs—but the booze was clouding her perception.

Paranoid drunks are the *worst*.

"What are we going to do?" Gemma cried, tugging frantically at the knob. She was tired, drunk, afraid, and come to think of it, *starving*. If they ever got inside, she wanted a grilled cheese sandwich.

"Try not to pull the thing off," America said, suddenly alert. She had a talent for sobering up under pressure.

"Step aside, ladies," Dana said valiantly, banging on the door with her foot and ramming her shoulder into its thick wooden frame. "Fuck, that really hurt," she laughed.

"Let's break it down!" Gemma screamed from behind them.

Yup, the paranoia had turned to schizophrenia.

Gemma took a step back and scratched her Gucci-sandaled foot against the hardwood floor like a bull. Both Dana and America stared in awe. They looked at each other for answers but there was nothing rational going on here. Gemma was about to run head first into an eighty-pound wooden door. And then she did it. She bolted past her bewildered friends, making a beeline for the door.

"Gemma, don't!" America screamed.

Dana and America both heard the metal click of the deadbolt unlocking and watched in horror as the door swung open. Even in the dark, the burly figure standing on the other side was clearly not five-foot-two Gabriella. The girls froze, but momentum wouldn't allow Gemma to stop in time and she went flying into the intruder's arms.

SEVEN

"I have a gun!" Dana screamed. "Don't move, or I'll shoot."

"Don't shoot!" Gemma and the burglar screamed in unison. They were tangled up like pretzels on the smooth, checkered-marble floor of the foyer.

Oh god, Gemma panicked, swatting wildly at her assailant. Like she wasn't freaking out enough, now she had to worry about Dana accidentally shooting her in the ass? She swung her leg in the air and scrambled to her feet.

"Help!" she screamed. It was still dark, but Gemma's eyes were beginning to adjust to the light. She limped over to Dana and America, looking over her shoulder at the burglar writhing on the floor.

"Damn," the intruder choked, grabbing onto an antique wooden table and pulling himself up. "You have a gun, Dana?"

He knew her *name*? Was this guy a psychic burglar?

Gemma panted like a Newfoundland, hugging herself to keep from shaking. "Shoot him!" she yelled, tugging Dana's arm urgently. She reached around in her purse for something that might double as a weapon. Where was that Mace her parents made her promise to carry?

Suddenly Gemma stopped. It occurred to her that she was the only one panicking. She closed her purse, furrowing her brow at her friends. America's hands were on her hips in a casually amused pose. And Dana—who was totally lying about the gun, by the way—actually started laughing.

Hello, is somebody going to fill me in? Gemma huffed silently.

"You asshole!" Dana laughed, slapping her bare knee. "You scared the shit out of us." She ran into the foyer and threw her arms around the guy wearing nothing but khaki cargo shorts. He hugged her back and the two of them just stood there laughing like it was the last ten seconds of *Murder, She Wrote.*

"Don't worry, sweetie," America said, patting Gemma on the shoulder. She walked into the foyer, turning on a row of track lights, and leaned casually against the table next to the supposed burglar. Fluttering her fingers in a coy wave, she said, "Hi Danny. It's been a long time."

"Look at *you*," Danny replied appreciatively. He extended his hand and America awkwardly accepted it, flashing a demure smile.

Awkward? That's a first.

"Gemma. If you're done pissing in your pants, this is my big brother. I mean *step*brother, Danny Crane." Dana pinched his cheek affectionately and he swatted her hand away. "Danny, this is my friend Gemma from Sun Valley."

"What's up, Gemma," Danny yawned. "Do you drunks want to move this party inside?" he asked, scratching his hairy armpit.

"I'm so fucking thirsty I could drink Lake Como," Dana complained, leading the way to the kitchen.

Gemma shut the heavy wooden door, locking the deadbolt with force. She tried to act like this was all *so* amusing, but she was still freaking out. Even if it was just Danny, for a good forty-five seconds she had seriously feared for her life.

And it really upset her that Dana and America were acting like they didn't care. Weren't they supposed to be her best friends? Well, Dana anyway. Slipping out of her heels, Gemma tucked them under her arm and followed the gang to the kitchen. There was no way she still wanted that grilled cheese sandwich.

"Dude, what are you even doing here?" Dana asked, walking to the sink and filling four glasses with water. "I figured you'd be yakuza by now. Stepbitch said you'd be in Tokyo till Christmas."

"You still call her *Stepbitch*?" Danny laughed. "Why not *Mommie Dearest*?"

"Come on now, there were never any wire hangers," Dana quipped, rolling her eyes. "But before your *lovely, fabulous* mother left for Australia, she didn't mention anything about you coming to town." She distributed the water and collapsed onto a chair next to Gemma.

"Hey, are you okay Gemma?" she asked, pushing Gemma's hair behind her ear.

Gemma had retreated into the crook of her elbow, hiding like a scared kitty. She looked up, surprised to see that Dana's eyebrows were furrowed with concern. "I was really freaked out before," she said. It was supposed to sound matter-of-fact, but she burst into tears.

"Oh sweetie," Dana and America cooed, rubbing Gemma's back reassuringly.

"That must have scared the crap out of you, huh?" Dana said.

Gemma smiled and wiped her tears away with the back of her hand. It was nice being coddled for a couple minutes. New York was harrowing enough with*out* tackling a would-be burglar on the floor. She deserved a little babying.

"What about *me*?" Danny whined from his seat across the table. "I'm the one who got punched in the nuts!"

The girls burst out laughing.

"Yeah," America said, crossing her arms inquisitively. She flashed Danny a pouty grin and whispered, "What *about* you?"

Can anyone else feel the mounting sexual tension?

Danny grinned and shook his head in an *I see you're up to your old tricks* kind of way. He clasped his hands together and stretched his arms out in front of him, showcasing his bulging biceps. "I'm still at Dad's Tokyo branch," he said, yawning again.

America nodded approvingly. What was the deal with these two? Even Gemma, tipsy and terrified, could spot the chemistry from a mile away.

"CFG's got me in NYC for a meet-and-greet with a couple clients this weekend," he told the girls. Well, he told America. "I work at Crane Financial Group," he added for Gemma's benefit—as if *anyone* didn't know the multi-billion-dollar hedge fund.

"Well, *su casa es su casa*," Dana offered. "Hope you don't mind sharing the place with three sexy sophisticated schoolgirls."

"Are you kidding?" Danny smiled. He stood up, put his empty glass in the sink, and walked toward the kitchen door. "That's what I'm gonna call my barely legal website. A few strategically placed cameras, some eager pedophiles, a PayPal account, and voilà—instant fortune."

"Instant jail time," America replied, flipping Danny off. She blew a sarcastic kiss in his direction and he caught it, loping out of the room.

"He's kidding," she added, rubbing Gemma's arm.

Gemma forced a smile and walked to the sink. She seriously needed to go to bed. Waving good night over her shoulder, she pulled her exhausted body up the stairs and to her room. It was almost five a.m. and she had way too much information to process. A new *male* roommate who wanted to put her on a kiddie-porn website?

He'd *better* be kidding.

EIGHT

"Where are all the PAs?" James, Mr. Sleazy Smile, barked. No smiling today, however. He was a man on a mission.

"Mikayla's down in the studio," Gemma said, looking up from the blinding light of the copy machine. "And Chet and Bobby are out doing an MOS for Deniece."

MOS—short for "Man on the Street" interview—was Gemma's vocab word of the day. The boys were cruising Broadway with a video camera and boom microphone, release forms, and the question "What would you do for a million dollars?"

Kind of uninspired, don't you think?

"Can we help you with something?" Maria butt in from over near the fax machine.

Bitch, Gemma scowled.

James's face soured, but he tilted his head and examined the three interns. "Are you any good at research?" he asked, playing with a gold chain around his neck.

"Yes," all three girls responded on top of each other. "Research" was kind of a vague term, but no way was Gemma going to let the evil twins beat her to it.

"We're booking the 'Teenage Prostitutes' show. Go ask Carla and Kamara what you can do to help." James quickly turned and hurried out of the room.

Gemma grabbed a notepad and pen and shot Maria a surreptitious grin before speeding down the hallway. The race was on. Ballet flats gave Gemma the upper hand, and she dashed across the finish line and into Carla's office a whopping three seconds before the twins.

Three seconds, shmee seconds. It was an unequivocal victory.

"James sent me," she said, a little breathless. "What can I do to help?"

Carla didn't take her eyes off her computer screen. "Can you use LexisNexis?"

"I know it really well." Gemma silently thanked her English teacher for getting her to join the school paper junior year.

"Me too," Maria jumped in a little too late. She just looked like a suck-up.

"Okay. I need a teen prostitute. The younger the better."

That's not something you hear every day.

"Or good organizations that might be able to get us one," Carla added. "Look for really over-the-top stories, anywhere in the U.S. Print out whatever you find and give it to Kamara." She ripped a Post-it note off a larger stack and jotted down her LexisNexis ID and password, "Can you guys share this?" she asked.

"Sure," Anita said sweetly, grabbing the Post-it with lightning speed. She waved it in the air victoriously and ran back down the hall, Gemma and Maria close behind. None of them said anything, but it was so obviously a race.

Gemma sat down at a free computer, pulling up the LexisNexis home page. "Can I have Carla's ID and password, please?" she asked Anita, flashing a saccharine smile.

"Of *course*," Maria purred, ripping the Post-it out of Anita's hands and handing it over in a grand gesture.

Gemma entered the information and handed the Post-it back to Maria, batting her eyelashes and smiling like a little angel. *Two can play at that game.* Then she turned back to face her computer like this was *Mission: Impossible* and she had ten seconds to dismantle a bomb. She punched in a string of key words: runaway, girl, pimp, (sex w/3 money), hooker, prostitut!, teen!

The exclamations and parentheses were LexisNexis shortcuts. Then she narrowed her search parameters to only display articles from the last six to twelve months. And ... *go!*

Her stubby little fingers danced over the keys for the next two hours. Every time she hit "print" the thrill of accomplishment surged through her body. But she wasn't exactly winning. Every time she heard Anita or Maria print out an article her stomach sank a little. She desperately wanted to beat them.

"Hey."

The girls looked up. It was Timothy, the youngest producer on staff. He had this old-fashioned-movie-star thing going on, if for no other reason than he wore white chinos and sweater vests. He licked his fingertips delicately and leafed through *Us Weekly*, pausing on one page in particular with an inquisitive frown. "I need help with my show," he drawled, still ogling the latest celebrity scandal. "The show's about trends, and I need some eager little beavers to hit the streets and do some reconnaissance."

Gemma drummed her fingers on her mouse pad and bit her lip. She was torn. Finding hot new trends sounded killer, but she was kind of engrossed in the whole prostitution thing. Plus, Timothy's arrogant smirk, anal-retentive wardrobe, and condescendingly fake tone made her uneasy. Why should she kowtow when presumably the twins would be all over it?

And they were. "I'll do it!" they yelled, ditching their computers for Timothy. Maria flashed Gemma a nanny-nanny-boo-boo look, to which Gemma merely rolled her eyes. *Whatever*, she thought with a shrug, *less competition*.

However, it was a bittersweet victory. While the twins were window-shopping at Saks and Sanrio, Gemma read about prostitutes as young as twelve. The articles were depressing and useless. All the girls had generic names like "Ann" or "Mary" for anonymity. And if it wasn't *that* roadblock, they were homeless and didn't have contact information. A few of the articles listed specific teen shelters so Gemma printed those out and took her measly stack down the hall to Kamara.

"Thanks," Kamara said, pulling a pen out of her silky black ponytail. "Keep looking, okay?"

"Sure," Gemma nodded. She turned toward the door, then stopped. "Hey, Kamara, what's the lineup for this show?" The twins weren't on her back anymore so she had a couple minutes to kill.

Kamara pointed to an outline pinned to her corkboard. "There's an ex-prostitute who's trying to set up an employment-slash-tutoring program for young prostitutes. And a family therapist—therapists are a talk show staple. We've also got this super-nice couple whose daughter was killed by her pimp. It's a sweet lineup, but James and Penelope won't rest till we find an actual prostitute." She sighed in frustration, pointing to a stack of articles. "It's so pointless. What thirteen-year-old girl wants to go on TV and tell the world she's a hooker?"

"Good point," Gemma giggled uncomfortably. She looked at the show lineup again and perused the other items on Kamara's corkboard: her picture with Kate Morgan, a *Weekly World News* article about Bat Boy, a D.A.R.E. bumper sticker. Cute, kitschy stuff.

"What about money? Don't some shows pay their guests to come on TV?"

"Yeah," Kamara nodded. "Like, fifty bucks for eating expenses. But our really ghetto guests just spend the money on gear. You know—drugs, clothes, stuff like that. James has me looking for something other than money as a give-away, too. It just depends on who we get, what her hopes and dreams are, blah, blah, blah."

Sound *less* sincere.

"Right," Gemma nodded. Was everyone at *Back Talk* this jaded? How depressing. "Back to the grind," she said, suddenly desperate to get out of Kamara's fluorescent, airless office. She waved goodbye and backed into the hallway.

Maybe she was sick and twisted, but Gemma couldn't wait to get back to pimps and prostitutes. It was so depressingly tawdry. She loved it.

BACK TALK

Gemma had to do a double take, but it was true. The guy next to her on the subway was reading an article called *Teen Prostitutes: Our Future Leaders?*

Coincidence?

A giggle escaped from her mouth—not that it was funny, just ironic. She looked up to apologize for her inappropriateness and froze. It was the flirty Jonathan-Rhys-Meyers Subway Guy. Gemma cleared her throat and fiddled with her hands. She cursed her face for turning bright red as Subway Guy stared at her, his lips curling in a confused half smile.

"Are you all right?" Had he spoken with an English accent last time she saw him? Well, he did now, and it didn't get much sexier than that in Gemma's opinion. She pointed down at his magazine, speechless.

"Right," he said, clueless. "Prostitutes. Are you..."

"NO!" Gemma blurted out. *Cute British Subway Guy thinks I'm a hooker!*

She shook her head, burying her head in her hands. This was mortifying. She was totally overreacting, but it felt like everyone in the subway car was staring at her.

"Oh, I didn't mean *that.*" Now it was his turn to blush. "I was just going to say 'are you all right,' though I suppose I've already said that."

Gemma looked up at him from between her fingers. "I'm fine," she smiled. His accent made her little heart go pitter-pat. "I was only laughing because I've been looking for prostitutes all day," she told him.

A look of sheer horror flashed across Subway Guy's face.

"Oh god!" Gemma slapped her hands against her fiery red cheeks. "I don't mean *I* was looking for prostitutes."

Normally she wouldn't talk to strangers, but (a) she had to extricate her foot from her mouth, (b) she was never going to become a real New Yorker if she didn't loosen up a little, and (c) he was hot.

"I work at *Back Talk with Kate Morgan.* You know, the talk show? All day I've been reading depressing teen prostitution articles to find a guest for a show."

Gemma let out a sigh of relief when he smiled. He looked down at the article and laughed softly. "Oh, right. That sounds wicked," he said. He held out the magazine and arched his eyebrows. "Do you want it?"

Gemma felt butterflies in her stomach. "Oh, that's okay. Thanks," she blushed.

"Seriously," he urged. "I'm done with it. If it'll be of some use..."

"Thanks." Gemma smiled and took the magazine. She couldn't get over his deep, almond-shaped brown eyes. The subway stopped and they both stood up, walking onto the platform. Gemma slung her bag over her shoulder and walked slowly toward the stairs.

"Cheers, then. And good luck with your prostitute search," he said, taking the steps two at a time. "See you around the subway then, yeah?"

Gemma nodded and watched him disappear onto the street. As soon as he was gone she jumped up and down in a brief victory dance. Sure, she'd spazzed the beginning of their encounter—try Guinness Book of Lameness—but it had turned into a decent conversation. *Go me!* Gemma smiled.

She walked onto the street, too giddy to go straight home. The warm evening air tickled her skin and she turned left to take a quick detour through Central Park. She was still reeling. *And maybe*, she thought, taking long, thoughtful strides, *next time I see Subway Guy I'll be confident and smooooooth.*

It was a fun thought, anyway.

BACK TALK

"Hey, guys," Gemma waved as she walked into the living room. She tried not to puke, watching America and Danny giggling on the sofa. Yes, apparently her prediction of chemistry between the pair had been accurate.

"Hi Gemma," America giggled, looking up with a dreamy grin on her face. "Danny is telling me about his latest merger in Tokyo. You're such hot shit," she added, shoving him lightly.

"Yeah," Danny joked. He stood up, slipping his feet into Adidas flip-flops. "I've got to get going. I'm taking clients to the revolving restaurant at the Marriott Marquis tonight."

"The revolving restaurant?" America repeated incredulously. "Followed by the *ice* capades?"

Gemma laughed along with them, missing the irony but not wanting to be left out. She peeled off her baby blue Old Navy blazer and collapsed onto one of the suede sofas.

"I'll call you," Danny mouthed to America, backing out of the room. Ugh.

As soon as he was out of earshot, Gemma rolled onto her stomach and propped up on her elbows, cupping her chin with her hands. "Guess what!"

America rolled her eyes but smiled. "What?" she asked, taking the bait. It was fun having such an All-American "girlfriend."

"I saw Subway Guy again today!"

"Ooh," America cooed. She picked up her glass of iced coffee and leaned closer. "Give me the scoop."

Gemma jumped up and ran to sit next to America. Pulling her knees into her chest, she began retelling the story, word for word. Things were really starting to warm up between the two of them. Ever since their Friday night drunk-fest at Slip, Gemma had found her a lot less intimidating.

"Giving you the magazine was a nice gesture," America said, mulling over the facts. "*And* he hopes to see you again on the subway, which is good ..."

Gemma's heart sank, anticipating a "but."

"Maybe it's nothing," America hesitated. "But why didn't he ask for your number, or your name, or even tell you *his* name?"

Gemma folded her arms across her chest, suddenly feeling self-conscious. She hadn't even noticed the lack of name swapping. Was it really a big deal?

Eventually it might pose some problems ...

"I bet his name's Simon or Nigel," Gemma mused, choosing to make light of America's comment. "Those are such English names."

"Hold on," America snapped, sitting up on her knees. "Give me the magazine."

Gemma furrowed her brow suspiciously. What was America up to? She was really killing Gemma's buzz. But, what harm could it do? With a sigh, Gemma reached for her bag and dug the magazine out. America snatched it away and ran her finger down the cover. Why did she have to be so businesslike about the whole thing? Couldn't she just squeal a lot and be giddy like Gemma's friends back home?

America wasn't much for the squealing, and to be honest, Gemma's story was about a 0.2 on the wow-o-meter.

"Marcus Teller," she sang triumphantly, pointing at the lower right-hand corner of the magazine. "133 West Tenth Street."

Way to go, Veronica Mars.

"Do you think that's really him?" Gemma gushed.

America's immaculate face soured. "I don't know. Why would he take the A to Eighty-First if he lives in the West Village?"

Gemma sank down on the couch. America was being *such* a party pooper! "So you don't think this means anything?" she sighed, flopping onto the floor dramatically. How had she gone from cloud nine to complete despair in less than ten minutes?

"Sorry," America said.

Her sympathy sounded heartfelt, but Gemma wasn't sure America even knew what she was apologizing for. Reaching into her bag again, Gemma pulled out a bottle of water and sipped nervously. Her subway story was starting to feel pretty lame, especially when she compared it to the obvious romance between America and Danny.

"Can I ask you something?" Gemma said, waiting for America's nod to continue. "Does it make you nervous to date an older guy?"

"Danny's twenty-one," America answered matter-of-factly.

"Right," Gemma nodded and smiled awkwardly.

"It's not like we're 'dating,'" America said. She always used air quotes to trivialize and belittle. "He lives in Tokyo for god's sakes. If it were Paris..." A devilish smile crept across her face. She reached onto the coffee table for a bottle of nail polish remover and a bag of cotton balls. "Danny's great on paper: looks, charm, working his way up the corporate ladder. He's the perfect guy to show off to your parents.

Don't tell Dana I said that, okay?" America added, dunking a cotton ball in acetone.

"Of course not!" Gemma blurted before she could stop herself.

"I like Danny, I just can't *like* like him," she explained, badly. "It's great that he showed up in New York, but I know Dana's really overprotective of him. She'd kill me if she thought I was using him—which I'm not," she added, putting her cotton balls up defensively.

Gemma shrugged in agreement, unable to speak. Maybe she was too immature to get it, but she was having a hard time reading between the lines. Did America *not* like Danny? It kind of sounded that way. And that would be fine if he wasn't Dana's brother, but he was, and Gemma had loyalties.

The smell of acetone jolted her back to reality and Gemma sank down into the sofa, watching intensely as America dabbed her fingernails in a delicate circular motion.

NINE

"*Back Talk with Kate Morgan,* hold please. *Back Talk with Kate Morgan* ... I'll transfer you.*"

Blah, blah, *blah.* Gemma grumpily slammed the receiver down for the hundredth time and rolled her eyes. She'd been clicking from one line to the next nonstop while Melissa took her lunch break. It was beyond boring and just a *liiittle* bit creepy. Nut-jobs called in regularly with totally harebrained show ideas. Her favorite so far: "Do a blind date show where Kate Morgan goes to dinner with a dude from every state and the winner gets a million bucks and a lap dance!" Puke. Gemma longed for the days of researching teen prostitutes. Sure it was depressing, but it was also really interesting—and a lot better than listening to psychos all day. Her left ballet flat slid off her foot and she tapped her bare toe against the floor impatiently. When was something interesting going to happen? She glimpsed at the clock on her computer screen and sighed, barely able to believe she'd been sitting there for less than an hour.

"I'm in *The Parent Trap from Hell!*" James exploded, whipping through the reception area like a tornado. "They're *so* unprofessional."

Gemma's ears perked at the sound of gossip. Zipping up her black cotton hoodie, she sank down in her chair and watched as Talia, the gorgeous brunette supervising producer, struggled in four-inch Steve Madden heels to keep up. James stopped by a potted palm, fondling his jaw and looking frazzled and exhausted. He looked almost human—shock of all shocks.

A lovers' spat? Gemma mused as Talia finally caught up. She bent over to catch her breath and pull up her red halter top. Then with a bling-clad hand, she caressed James's shoulder, whispering in his ear. Gemma leaned closer. She was dying to know what they were talking about.

Come on—*The Parent Trap from Hell* didn't give it away?

"They won't leave me alone!" James whispered as the veins in his temples flexed convulsively. "I thought giving them an assignment would get them off my back but they took it as an invitation. They were sitting on my *desk* when I got to work this morning, Tal. Are they hitting on me or just trying to drive me insane? Either way," he paused and nodded cordially as Val walked through the room on her cell phone. "I'm about to go postal!" He banged his fist against the wall then retracted it gingerly, regretting the burst of aggression. "If it wasn't for their god damned father I'd—"

"James, not here!" Talia whispered curtly. She jerked her head toward the front desk and Gemma blushed as their eyes fell on her.

"*Back Talk with Kate Morgan*, can I help you?" she squeaked, quickly picking up the phone and talking to the dial tone. She flashed James a mousy smile, playing with the knotted phone chord. Suddenly she felt uneasy. Did they know that she'd been listening? Did she even know what she'd heard? If she didn't know, would they think she did? Was it something bad?

Jesus Christ. Somebody give this girl a Xanax.

"I need a cigarette," James decided. His eyes lingered on Gemma as he fumbled in his pocket for a pack of Marlboros. Ick. The tuft of black hair poking out of his unbuttoned gray Thomas Pink shirt made her want to vomit. "Ready?" He turned and put his palm on Talia's shoulder blade, then looked back at Gemma, sending her a playful wink. Hard to believe that the guy with the obtrusive chest wig and wandering eye was complaining about being hit on. Puh-lease.

Gemma shuddered as they left the reception area, feeling a little bit like she needed a shower. But she was curious. If he was bitching about the Olsen twits maybe he was a halfway decent guy. From the sound of it, Maria and Anita were pulling some creepy *Fatal Attraction* shit on him. Nobody deserved *that*.

TEN

"Where are you going, Alias?" Clark asked, falling into step with Gemma.

"Home," Gemma sighed, fishing some Blistex out of her bag. She pressed the down button and leaned against the elevator doors, smiling at Clark. He looked adorable in a faded yellow Cheerios T-shirt and pressed jeans. It would never have occurred to Gemma in a billion years to press a pair of jeans.

"I'm going home, too," Clark yawned. "I was so bored today I actually read *Newsweek*." He took Gemma's hand and sluggishly pulled her away as the elevator doors swung open. It was packed, but they were determined to squeeze on.

"Well, lookie here," a deep voice murmured from behind Gemma as they began their downward descent.

The hair on the back of Gemma's neck stood up when she realized who it was. Nick's Acqua Di Gio was becoming quite the familiar scent. She cringed, suddenly remembering that she hadn't seen him since her tongue was in his ear at Slip on Friday night. Ah, memories. Taking a shaky breath, Gemma slowly turned her head, smiling at him like she *wasn't* about to die of embarrassment.

Kill me now. Gemma turned to face the elevator doors. She pushed a loose strand of brown hair behind her ear and bit her lip. Her eyes levitated skyward, combing the shiny brass elevator ceiling for a conversation topic.

Ding. The doors swung open on the eighth floor and Gemma stepped back, knowing that her body must be half an inch from Nick's. She pretended not to notice his warm Altoid breath on the back of her right ear.

Stay calm, Gemma ordered, gripping the hem of her denim shorts. *Shorts!* She rolled her eyes, cursing *Back Talk*'s lax dress code for enabling her to look like such a dork.

"Hasta mañana," Nick said with a nod as the elevator opened onto the lobby. He took a few steps then stopped to look back at Gemma, a lazy grin dancing on his lips. The fact that he knew he was so gorgeous should probably have deterred her, but it didn't. Finally, Nick shook his head with smug satisfaction and disappeared through the revolving doors. Swoon.

"What was *that* about?" Clark asked, bringing Gemma back down to earth. He mumbled something incoherent and slid his toned arm through Gemma's, ushering her out of the building.

"Nothing!" Gemma squeaked.

They walked onto the sidewalk and Gemma closed her eyes, reveling in the warm evening air. The sweet smoky aroma of caramelized peanuts was sickeningly addictive. For one solid minute Gemma wanted to forget about boys and her awkward social dysfunctions and just be one with na-ture—like *that's* possible in Manhattan.

"What are you doing here?" Gemma giggled as she opened her eyes, spotting America and Dana under a tree. They looked painfully inconspicuous. Dana's low-rise cam-ouflage cargo pants and skintight black halter top were okay, but America had to be sweating balls in that black ve-lour monogrammed Juicy sweat suit. Both ensembles were capped off with huge Jackie O. sunglasses and stylish yet sensible shoes.

Double-0-Divas, coming this fall on ABC . . . think about it.

"Hot much?" Gemma asked, tiptoeing up to her friends. She put her hand across Clark's shoulder blades. "This is Clark, from work. Clark, meet Dana and America."

"The infamous roommates!" Clark sang giddily. He leaned forward and whispered, "Are we planning a heist? I have an army-print bandana up on my desk if you need it."

"We stick out?" America asked flatly. The espionage gear had *not* been her idea. "It's nice to meet you, Clark. Gemma says you're the bee's knees."

"Likewise. But seriously, what are you up to?"

Dana scanned for spies, then gathered everyone in for a huddle. "Do you know about Subway Guy?"

Clark nodded. Gemma had regaled him with the details over Diet Cokes and a faxing marathon.

"We're gonna do a little recon," Dana continued, "and find the address on the magazine he gave her the other day."

"We are *not!*" Gemma gasped in horror. She shook her head vehemently. "I'm not a stalker. I refuse to traipse through New York with a bunch of incognito freaks."

Suddenly the refreshing summer air felt suffocating and thick. This was worse than the infamous eighth grade dance fiasco. The fact that her parents had chaperoned was mortifying enough, but when her dad stole the mic for a duet with the principal? *Biiig* therapy bill. And "Gettin' Jiggy Wit It" still gave Gemma nightmares.

She shuddered, trying to repress the heinous memory. "Forget it," she said, stamping the sidewalk for added dramatic flair. "I embarrass myself enough by accident, I don't need to seek out humiliation."

"Dude, don't get your panties in a twist," Dana huffed, pulling a cigarette out of her leather Kooba bag and lighting it with a match from the Soho Grand Hotel. "It's not like we're going to kick the mo'fo's door down. It's just recon."

"It'll be fun," America urged. "Besides, I left the auction house early today for this, so you better do it."

"*You* went to work today?" Gemma asked.

If by "work" she meant gallery hopping followed by a facial at Bliss, then yes.

Gemma puffed out her lower lip, blowing air upward to cool her face. It was sweet of her friends to be so interested in her love life, but this had an eerily NBC-sitcom feel to it. She squinted thoughtfully, looked deep into Dana's eyes, then America's. Even Clark looked gung-ho. Et tu, Clark?

"Only if Clark comes," Gemma surrendered. She wasn't as annoyed as she sounded. In fact, she was even a teensy bit excited. She hadn't played detective since she was, like, ten.

"Right on," Dana whooped. She put her fingers to her lips and whistled for a cab while America applauded Gemma with a demure golf clap.

Gemma shook her head miserably. She was mortified already, but what could she do? A minivan cab screeched to a halt in front of them and they piled in, sailing down Seventh Avenue on a mission.

BACK TALK

The butterflies in Gemma's stomach multiplied by the hundreds as the taxi neared Tenth Street. Suddenly she couldn't remember why she'd agreed to this. What if Subway Guy saw her? With her camouflaged cohorts in tow there was no chance of it looking like a coincidence. She bunched her brown frizz into a rubber band and blotted her forehead with a Cover Girl compact.

Don't forget to breathe.

"Stop here," America ordered the cabby. She handed him a twenty and nodded across the street while she waited for change. "There it is, guys."

Metro Records. It was a store? Gemma dragged her heels along the sidewalk, a little disappointed. During the fifteen-minute cab ride she'd concocted this dazzling image: a picturesque little brownstone complete with quaint English topiary and Subway Guy himself, lounging on the stoop sipping espresso and mulling over a copy of *The Village Voice*.

Yuck. Sounds like a John Mayer video.

Gemma scratched her knee, feeling as country-bumpkinish as ever next to the chic hipsters in their vintage threads and retro coiffures. From the safety of a telephone booth across the street, she peered into the shop's window, spotting indie posters and used CDs. Who the hell were all those bands? Apparently Gemma's taste wasn't as eclectic as she thought.

"What do we think," Clark asked, twiddling his thumbs. "Are we going in?"

"Damn straight," Dana sang, grabbing Gemma's arm before she could protest.

"No," Gemma whimpered, but she was already halfway across the street.

"Don't be nervous," America instructed. She pinched Gemma's cheeks and smoothed down her hair. "This is a record shop. They *want* you to go in. It's your patriotic duty as a consumer. It's for our country!" she enthused with bulging eyes. "Besides," she added, regaining her usual aloof composure, "I've been looking for an old Belle and Sebastian EP."

Gemma cupped her hands over her heart and smiled. Seeing America display enthusiasm was like watching a kid learn to read. But Gemma was getting off track. With a troubled sigh she rolled her shoulders and glanced inside the shop. The rational pros and cons weighed heavily in favor of Gemma running for the hills, but she had to admit she was curious.

"Fuck it. Let's go in."

ELEVEN

Gemma leaned back and popped another Oreo into her mouth. She chomped morosely, washing it down with a tangy '03 Sancerre. Wine wasn't really her thing, but America swore it was a good vintage, and it got the job done. She took another sip and let it ease down her throat as she thought about Subway Guy, *some more*. At first she'd been relieved that he wasn't at Metro Records. Then she'd felt slightly disappointed. By the time they dropped Clark off in Chelsea she'd almost reached acceptance, but now, after half a bottle of wine and five too many cookies, she was regressing.

"Would you stop *eating*?" Dana spat, grabbing the nearly empty bag of Oreos and throwing them across the room. "I'm getting fat just watching you."

"What is your damage, Heather?" America was drunk in solidarity and slurring *Heathers* quotes left and right. Somebody stop her before she tries to say "'*ich lüge*' bullets."

"I'm sorry," Dana grumbled, refilling her glass and sucking it down. "But I'm depressed, too, and you don't see me drowning my sorrows in cookies."

No, just small fermented grapes from the Loire Valley.

"What's wrong?" Gemma asked, trying to mask her embarrassment. *I wasn't the only one eating cookies*, she pouted silently.

"I feel like an asshole," Dana said, letting out an electrifying sigh. "Remember that DJ I told you about. The one I met last week? Well, I saw him in Soho today."

America nodded, playing with a strand of luminous pearls around her neck.

"I went up to say hi to him."

"You *did*!" Gemma cried, giggling like a schoolgirl. "Sorry," she added, clearing her throat.

Dana twirled a blonde curl around her index finger and continued. "All I said was hi, and he stood there staring at me like a fucking retard," she yelled, cradling her head dramatically. She raised her palm in the air as if remembering a major detail. "Oh, and it gets better. The assholes he was with? They burst out *laughing* at me!"

"*No*," America gasped in horror. Being laughed at was worse than wearing last season's bubble skirt at fashion week.

She grabbed the bottle and filled Dana's glass to the brim. "What an ass. He didn't say *any*thing?"

Gemma nodded, wanting to know the same thing. She leaned closer, fishing an ice cube out of her glass, and popped it in her mouth.

"I took off before he had a chance," Dana snorted. In one motion she unhooked her bra, sliding it out from under her Marc Jacobs polka-dot tank and flung it across the room. "Don't all console me at once," she said, laughing uncomfortably.

Gemma smiled in spite of the situation. Knowing that even beautiful people get embarrassed suddenly gave her a sick sense of relief. "What a dick. You deserve way better than that," she said, squeezing Dana's knee. "I can't believe you didn't burst into tears. If that happened to me I would have pissed in my pants."

Dana laughed, grabbing Gemma's head for a noogie. "Well, thank god for me, I know how to control my bladder!" She pushed herself off the sofa, obviously ready to move on. "I smell chili. Come on, let's see what Gabby's making."

Gemma agreed, stifling a hiccup as she walked toward the door. She glanced at the framed Warhol print of Marilyn Monroe in the hallway, noticing her own Oreo-crumb-stained reflection. She furtively brushed the crumbs away, still bruised by Dana's cookie comment. Sure it was harsh, but how did Gemma *think* Dana got that body? Spin class?

Yeah, that and Dr. Miller on Park Ave.

TWELVE

"Gemma, thank god you're here!" Simone screamed. Her black Diane Von Furstenberg wrap dress flapped open at her thighs as she ran toward Gemma, a desperate look on her face.

Great. What crap task was Gemma going to be asked to do now? She'd already organized the supply closet and redrawn the calendar on the dry erase board. She peeled off her vintage Levi's jacket, managing to fling it over a chair as Simone grabbed her hand and whisked her down the hall to the audience department where the people Clark had described as horny chain smokers dwelled.

"Neela," Simone barked to a petite Indian woman with curly black hair.

Neela's head sprang up faster than a jack-in-the-box, her wiry curls bouncing up and down long after she'd stopped moving.

"You get Gemma this morning." Simone shoved Gemma into the over-air-conditioned room and ran out, slamming the door shut behind her.

Nice escape.

Gemma stood there in her yellow cotton halter dress, stroking her shoulders for warmth. How could the audience department be *this* freezing when it was like Saudi Arabia in the PA room?

"What can I do?" she asked, forcing a smile at Neela and her two assistants. Maybe it was just Neela's dark skin in comparison, but the other two girls—in drab Ann Taylor dresses, jabbering a mile a minute into oversized headsets—looked gaunt and pasty. Gemma wanted to treat them each to a Snickers and ten minutes at E-Z Tan.

"I need you to help Enid," Neela commanded, pointing to a high-strung plain Jane in her twenties. "Enid!" she screamed, prompting the thin, stringy blonde to scurry over.

"Lovely of you to help," she chirped in a posh London accent. "Gemma was it? I'm afraid what we're doing won't be terribly fun..." She scooped a large stack of pink, green, and yellow flyers into her arms and smiled energetically. "So, Deniece is producing a wacky careers show today," she said, linking arms with Gemma and ushering her out of the icebox.

Gemma nodded, peering down out of the corner of her eye at their intertwined arms. She wasn't, like, *anti*-PDA, but how long had she known Enid? Twenty-five seconds? They weren't exactly BFF. Enid dragged Gemma down the hallway, stopping briefly in the supply closet for a Polaroid camera and extra film, a stapler, and a handful of pens. Gemma frowned, trying to piece together the clues. Were they going to play Pictionary?

"We need to get audience members to fill out this questionnaire," Enid continued, walking toward the elevator and ramming her thumb against the down button. "It's loaded with lame questions like 'My dream career is...' and 'Nuttiest job I ever had was...' That type of thing." She pulled Gemma into the elevator and ripped one of the film cartridges open with her teeth. "Shoot me for sounding insensitive, but we only want young, good-looking responses. Can you manage?" she asked, loading the film into the camera. "For instance: Brad Pitt or Woody Allen?"

Gemma stared at Enid, her mouth agape with confusion.

"Come on," Enid prodded, snapping her fingers. "If two blokes are standing there, give the questionnaire to the one that looks like Brad Pitt. No offense, Woody's a genius, but nobody wants to look at *that*."

Gemma laughed.

"Okay," Enid smiled, walking down the hallway. "See all those people?"

Gemma nodded. The mile-long line was hard to miss.

"It's today's audience," Enid explained. She handed Gemma the camera, stapler, and pens, keeping a few questionnaires and a pen for herself. "Come on, then. I'll show you how it's done."

Enid walked briskly toward the poor man's Charlize Theron and gave her a big wave hello. "Hi! I'm Enid with *Back Talk*. I've got a questionnaire for you to fill out. And," she added in a singsong voice, grabbing the camera from Gemma, "everyone who fills out the questionnaire gets her picture taken!"

Charlize clapped her hands, jumping up and down like a seal in her gray tube dress. She flashed a sexy smile for the camera, and then examined the questionnaire, tapping the pen against her lip as she contemplated her worst job interview ever.

"What are the Polaroids for?" Gemma asked, following Enid down the corridor.

"So Vince can find them for bumps."

Gemma paused, feeling like an idiot for having to ask, "What are bumps?"

"Sorry," Enid said, smacking her forehead. "You've met Vince, right? The director?"

Vince, the six-foot-five Viking dude, was hardly inconspicuous.

"At the end of segment one, Vince will have the camera operator pan to an audience member. Regina, for instance," she said, slapping the picture of Charlize. "Then the chyron operator will put up the answer to one of Regina's questions, like: Regina once fell asleep at a job interview. Chyrons are the fancy name for the factoids at the bottom of the screen. It's called a 'bump out' at the end of a segment, and a 'bump in' after the commercial break coming into a segment. Get it?"

"Got it."

"Good." Enid looked down at her watch. "I've got to get into the studio. You'll do fine. Just get about twenty really good responses."

Gemma nodded, heading down the line slowly. There wasn't a Brad among them, but halfway down, she spotted her first target: A tall, exotic black woman in white linen pants and a black knit tank top.

"Hi, would you fill out a questionnaire?" Gemma asked timidly. "And let me take your picture?"

"No," the woman roared, shoving her hands on her hips defiantly.

Reearrr.

Gemma bit her lip, not quite sure how to react. Like talking to people wasn't hard enough, this woman had to go and intentionally be a bitch.

"S-sorry," she mumbled, feeling her face turn the color of canned beets. Embarrassed and on the verge of tears, Gemma spun around on her blue straw flip-flops and fled to the bathroom to catch her breath. She took a few wet paper towels and blotted her face. No wonder the chicks in audience were chain smokers.

"Okay," Gemma cheered her reflection. She picked up her supplies and walked back into the crowd, cornering the first non-ugly woman that gave her a second glance.

"Hi. Will you please fill this out?" Gemma smiled meekly.

"Ooh, that sounds fun!" the pregnant Chinese girl cooed, taking the questionnaire. "Hey, can my husband fill it out, too?"

Gemma tilted her head, noticing the scrawny, fifty-something Jewish guy in thick glasses and a Mets cap. What was that Woody Allen thing again?

"Sure!" she replied through clenched teeth. Why be mean just to save a Polaroid and a sheet of paper? As they filled out the stupid, kitschy questionnaire, Gemma browsed the line for her next victim. Then she snapped Woody and Sun Yi's picture and continued.

Two down, eighteen to go.

BACK TALK

The faint whir of clapping caught Gemma's attention as she walked down the hallway. She tiptoed quietly toward the noise, peaking first into Nina's office and then James's. Gemma frowned. Why were Ms. O'Shea, Carla, Kamara, and the twins hovering around James's desk?

"Entrez," James called out in butchered French. "You were helping with the prostitution search, right? Well, look no further!" He clapped, gesturing to Anita and Maria.

Too easy.

Anita grinned like a jackass. "*We* saved the show," she beamed.

Gemma harrumphed, walking farther into the room. "Wow," she said, fighting the urge to puke. "That's great." Her eyes shifted around the room, landing on James. What was his deal? Two days ago the twins were driving him into early retirement, but now suddenly they were heroes? She held her elbows self-consciously, backing toward the door. If the twins *were* heroes, then she'd spent over three hours searching for a story that took them twenty minutes to find. She blushed at the thought.

"Carla called her and booked her last night," James told Penelope, wiping a few flakes of dandruff off his shiny black muscle shirt.

"You're gonna love her," Carla promised enthusiastically. She stood up from her seat in the corner and picked up a stack of magazines. "I should get started on her tape package."

"Great," Ms. O'Shea smiled, adding, "I'm sure *everyone* has work to do." She pulled a Kelly green pashmina around her shoulders and sucked heartily at her iced mochachino. "Let's talk bumps and teasers tomorrow a.m., James."

Gemma smiled, feeling oh-so-cool now that she knew what bumps were.

"Congrats, Carla," she said, trotting to catch up to her.

"Thanks," Carla smiled. She twisted her long caramel and chocolate extensions, tying them into a knot at the base of her neck and whispered, "I feel guilty, though. I told Ms. O'Shea our new prostitute is great, but *damn*. A bag of dirt makes better conversation."

"Really?" Gemma asked in awed fascination. "Is that bad?"

You try talking to a bag of dirt.

"The girl's got an eighth grade education, she's scared as hell, and she's got an abusive pimp breathing down her neck," Carla explained. She walked into her office, nodding for Gemma to follow her. "I'm not complaining, though. She's got a great story. Thank god Anita and Maria found it."

There it was again: praise for the twins. Gemma winced. "So what's next? Is there anything I can do to help?"

"Well, I've got to put together a tape package."

Gemma stared blankly.

"A *tape* package," Carla said again, rolling her eyes. "Sometimes Kate or the guests do voiceovers along with a home-video-slash-photo montage before their segment." She pulled a green folder out of her desk and rifled through its contents. "That's called a tape package. It's the sappiest Hallmark shit you'll ever hear, but it gets the point across. We tape them before the show in a sound booth we share with the morning news."

"Okay," Gemma nodded. She leaned against the wall, glancing at *All My Children* on mute behind Carla's head. Somebody was being threatened at knifepoint. "How do you know what to write?"

Carla found what she was looking for in the green folder and handed it to Gemma. "We use these. They're called pre-interviews," she said, enunciating slowly. "It's basically Q and A. Our head writer uses the pre's to write the script, and Kate Morgan uses them to brush up on the guests before the show."

"Wow, useful." Goosebumps prickled Gemma's skin as she mulled over her new vocabulary: chyrons, bumps, pre's ... It kind of evened out all the copying and filing. She pushed her body off the wall, looking back up at the TV for a second. Yup, somebody had been stabbed. "Well, if you need my help..." she trailed off, knowing that Carla didn't.

But Simone probably did, and Gemma would do almost anything to keep her mind off those deceitful, conniving, thunder-stealing twins. She was practically sick with doubt and envy. Could the twins really have found that article? *I guess it's possible*, Gemma pouted as she slunk down the hall. Maria got a fifteen hundred on her SATs, after all.

Bitch.

THIRTEEN

Gemma walked into the foyer, shutting and locking the front door behind her. The house looked and sounded empty, but she was determined to find her friends, *stat*. She flung her bag on an antique upholstered chair, glancing into the sitting room to her left, and walking down the hall to poke her head into the library on her right. Nada.

"Hello?" she called out, her voice echoing in the silence. "Anyone home?"

Gemma frowned, grabbing the mahogany banister and hurtling up the stairs. She stopped briefly to check the exercise room and informal den and then continued up. Her day had sucked—due in no small part to the twins' unjust victory—and now she wanted to do tequila shots, or at least eat one of those yummy chocolate cookies from Levain Bakery. Anything to get her mind off those hateful little snots.

"Dana?" she said, peeking into the A.P.C./Marc Jacobs war zone that was Dana's bedroom. An old Strokes video blasted out of her wall-mounted plasma TV, but there was no Dana.

"Damn it," Gemma huffed. No Dana meant no tequila shots.

With a grumpy moan, Gemma plodded down the hall toward America's bedroom. She crinkled her nose in disgust as she realized sweat was trickling down her back. Her pretty, yellow sundress was getting soaked and the stifling apartment was just adding to her horrendous mood. On top of everything else, she couldn't even *not* sweat!

She pushed America's door open, expecting to see nothing but fancy, expensive clothes. She wasn't that lucky.

"Holy shit!" Gemma screamed, shielding her virgin eyes.

She staggered backwards while Danny pulled an orange Egyptian cotton sheet over the bed. *Awkward!* Stumbling again, she tripped over a Michael Kors espadrille and fell face first on America's shag rug. Immediately she sprang to her feet, blushing at America and Danny. Then she stepped back, quickly pulling the door shut behind her.

"I'm really, really sorry!" Gemma yelled back, booking it down the hall.

Nice one, slick.

She ran into the living room and dove onto the couch, tucking her legs under her dress. The TV was already on but she grabbed the remote, madly surfing for something wholesome. Rachael Ray's obnoxiously perky face appeared before her on the Food Network and Gemma stared at a vat of fried chicken. She needed to purge the Kama Sutra from her brain.

"Are you scarred for life?" America asked, appearing in the doorframe in a yellow button-down Brooks Brothers shirt.

And underwear, Gemma hoped.

"Not scarred for *life*," she replied, forcing her eyes to meet America's. "Maybe just a few weeks."

Silence added to the awkwardness as America and Gemma stared at each other.

"Back when I was a kid, we ate raw garlic like it was popcorn!" Rachael Ray squawked from the TV. For a solid two minutes, her voice was the only one in the room.

Gemma chewed on her lower lip, pleating the fabric of her dress with her hands. The creepy awkwardness was mostly in her head, but she wondered if America felt embarrassed, too. Of course she did, but America was also in boarding school. The life of a boarder isn't exactly conducive to privacy. It's like Murphy's Law that you'll get walked in on at least once.

"The look on your face!" America finally said, laughing uncontrollably. She nestled down on the couch next to Gemma and grabbed a chocolate mint from the crystal candy dish on the coffee table.

"Come on," Gemma blushed. "Like you wouldn't have been embarrassed if the situation were reversed?" She threw a decorative pillow at America's shoulder and giggled. "Just be glad I wasn't Gabriella. You probably would have given her a heart attack!"

America nodded in agreement, shoving the pillow behind her back.

"So?" Gemma said expectantly. "What happened?"

America bit her lip—coated in Nars Orgasm lip-gloss, no less—and gave a coy shrug. America wasn't one to divulge those intimate details. She reached for another chocolate mint and popped it into her mouth.

"Oh my god, you have to tell!" Gemma screamed, giddily forgetting how nervous America made her. "Wait, so does this mean you actually *like* Danny?"

America frowned. "Wh—"

"I got it!" Dana shrieked, running into the living room in a Burberry string bikini and a cowboy hat.

"What are you talking about?" Gemma asked, giggling. Only Dana Cox could bounce into a room that confidently in two square inches of plaid.

"And where the hell did you *come* from?" America added dubiously.

"I was on the roof sunbathing," Dana replied matter-of-factly. That was where she spent most afternoons when she was skipping her Alexander Technique class. She catapulted over the sofa, landing clumsily between Gemma and America. Her skin was still warm from the sun and smelled like cocoa butter. "Didn't I tell you guys about my audition?" she asked, stretching her tan legs out on the coffee table. "My improv teacher got me an audition for this indie film. It's a first-time director and probably has a ridiculous budget of, like, a hundred thousand dollars or something, but the audition went well and one of the producers just called. They offered me a supporting role. I'm in a fucking movie! Am I amazing or what?"

Clearly she thought so.

"Wicked!" Gemma exclaimed, feigning as much excitement as possible. She was convinced: good things happened to everyone but her.

"Wow, Gemma, looks like we're in the presence of greatness," America said dryly. "Seriously sweetie, that's amazing. Kudos." She tucked her knees up inside Danny's shirt, pulling her disheveled hair into a low ponytail. "Now would you close your legs? You need a Brazilian, ASAP."

Dana gasped, covering her mouth in mock horror. "Bitch!" she screamed, throwing a gray cashmere blanket across her lap. "Satisfied?" she said, her voice laden with insincerity. "What about you, biatch? Like your outfit's *so* kosher." She fingered the monogrammed lapel of America's pale yellow button-down, a suspicious look creeping onto her face. "I know that shirt. Hold on. Did you ... ? No effing *way*, dude!"

"Yeah," America blushed jubilantly, sucking air between the tiny gap in her pearly white front teeth. "While you were exposing yourself to aerial photographers, I was, errr, practicing a little bedroom olympics with your brother."

Dana's eyes popped like flashbulbs. "Shut *up*!" she gasped, shoving America's shoulder. "You dirty whore! Okay, this story calls for pants. Don't talk till I get back."

Dana jumped off the sofa and tossed the cashmere blanket onto the floor. Her plaid bikini bottoms had ridden up her ass and she paused to pick her wedgie in America's face before skipping out of the living room. Charming.

"I thought you didn't even like Danny," Gemma asked in a low voice.

America's head shot toward the door. "What are you talking about?" she whispered curtly, looking back at Gemma.

"Last week!" Gemma whispered back. "All that stuff about Danny only looking good on paper—'I can't *like* like him.'"

America untucked her legs from Danny's shirt and shook her head, wondering why she'd confided in Gemma in the first place. Gemma knew as much about dating as America knew about plowing fields, or whatever they did in the heartlands. Grabbing the remote off the table, America raised the volume on the TV to ensure their privacy. "I know what I said," she snapped. "But are you sure *you* do?"

"I'm not trying to argue," Gemma mumbled, her face wrinkled in confusion. "But I know what I heard."

The frosty glare on America's face suggested otherwise.

"No," America whispered angrily. She shook her head in frustration. This was out of hand. "The problem—"

"What'd I miss?" Dana asked, appearing in the doorway in leopard print capris and a matching short-sleeved hoodie. It was one of those birthday present outfits from her stepbitch that she'd never be caught dead wearing in public, but was soft and comfy enough to throw on in the privacy of her own living room.

"Nothing," America lied. "Just telling Gemma the sappy details you won't want to hear." She crossed her legs over the arm of the sofa and shot Gemma a threatening look before smiling up at Dana.

"Like ...?" Dana asked, zipping up her hoodie. She found a root beer Dum-Dum in the pocket and peeled away the wrapper, shoving it in her mouth.

"Like ... Danny and I took a boat ride in Central Park today."

Dana shuddered and stuck the Dum-Dum down her throat, pretending to gag.

Gemma smiled nervously, avoiding America's glare as she made room for Dana on the sofa.

B A C K   T A L K

"Gemma," whispered a voice outside Gemma's bedroom door.

She looked at her bedside alarm clock. Eleven fifteen. She wasn't asleep yet, but she was in bed devouring *Entertainment Weekly* and not really in the mood for visitors. Tossing the magazine on her pillow, she slid out of bed, tiptoeing across the hardwood floor. Whatever whoever wanted, it better be quick, because Gemma needed her beauty sleep. She twisted the knob and Dana shot past her, hurrying toward the bed. The dark and furtive look on her face suggested "secret mission" but thankfully the black silk Vera Wang robe implied "night in."

"What was going on earlier?" she asked, flopping down on Gemma's bed and stuffing a lace bolster pillow under one arm.

"You're gonna have to be more specific," Gemma yawned, snuggling underneath the lilac-printed sheets she brought from home. She'd brought a few other reminders as well, like her tattered '80s Madonna poster, and Tex, the world's softest teddy bear.

"I'm not an idiot," Dana whispered, resentfully. Her lower lip quivered slightly as she looked down at her hands and sighed in self-pitying exasperation. "I know you and America were talking about me tonight," she pouted, tugging at Tex-the-teddy's stubby tail. "You know, when I left the room to change?"

Oh god. Gemma gulped. She really, *really* wanted to avoid this conversation. Maybe there was an escape route ... like the window.

Hello, three-story drop.

"Okay." Gemma sighed, lacing her fingers together on her lap. How was she going to put this ... "I think America's just using your brother."

Dana sat bolt upright and slammed the pillow against the bed. "What?"

"Shh!" Gemma begged. "You look like you're going to explode."

A fair assumption. Dana's dewy, caramel tan was splotched red with anger and her jaw had clenched tighter than a jar of pickles. The girl had serious rage issues. She shook her head slowly, having some kind of MacBethian moment and stared at her hands. Talk about psycho.

Suddenly Dana jumped off the bed, pacing around the room like a speed freak. She was outraged. She thought her friends had been talking shit about *her*—she was the first to admit she had issues—but this threw her for a loop. Danny was a good brother, all things considered, and she refused to let some rich bitch screw him over.

Oh please. Like *she* didn't use men.

"That bitch!" Dana seethed. "I'll kill her."

She looked like she meant it, too, which was a little creepy.

"Retract fangs, Cujo," Gemma said lightheartedly. "And please don't say anything. America made me promise not to tell you. Besides, maybe I'm wrong. She looked pretty happy when she was talking about Danny tonight."

"Mm-hmm," Dana grumbled. She stopped in front of Gemma's dresser and reached underneath, fumbling around until she pulled out a pack of Marlboro Lights. Was there a single room in her house that *didn't* have a secret stash of cigarettes?

"I hope you're right," she murmured, resting a cigarette between her lips and puffing on it, unlit.

"Uh-huh." Gemma smiled uncomfortably, waiting for Dana to breathe fire or sprout horns or something.

"Listen," Dana said, walking to the door. She looked poised and confident, like a litigator. "I just decided I'm not talking to her. You don't have to tell her why or anything, but I can't deal with that rich bitch right now." She opened the door and angrily flipped off the hallway in the direction of America's bedroom. Then she turned and smiled. "Good night, Gem."

Yeah, sweet friggin' dreams.

FOURTEEN

Gemma folded a neon green flyer and stuffed it in a white *Back Talk* envelope. Sigh. Just when she thought she'd done every boring job on the planet, Simone stuck her with something even lamer. Chucking the envelope in a box, Gemma reached across the table for another flyer, creasing it with her teeth for variety.

On the bright side, at least she wasn't doing a reenactment. Nina's date rape show had gone way over budget so they couldn't hire actors for her blurry, dimly lit dramatization. That meant Maria and Chet had to do it instead. Just imagine simulating rape in a crammed Honda while a producer and a cameraman critique you from the back seat. God, what a nightmare.

Gemma hummed a Gwen Stefani song as she crossed and uncrossed her legs. Her wool pants were totally chafing and she was desperate for a shopping spree. *Yeah, in the Dumpster.* This whole nonpaying internship thing was cramping her style. She shook her head mournfully, contemplating the inevitable: groveling for cash from the 'rents. Puh-thetic.

"I'm *sorry*, James," someone sniveled.

Gemma slid down in her seat as James ran into Hell with Kamara at his heels. The man did *not* look pleased. Sweat stains and rosacea trumped his usual *GQ* looks and there was a maniacal, Disney-villainish glow in his dark eyes.

"Not good enough!" he screamed. "We're going to be here till midnight because of you." He blotted his disgustingly sweaty brow with his hand, wiping the excess liquid on the back of his tight Diesel jeans.

"I was on a personal errand," Kamara panted. Puffy red splotches dotted her nose and cheeks and she looked like she might pee in her white Theory capris.

James folded his arms testily, waiting for her to continue. What a dick. Gemma couldn't believe he was berating her in public like this.

"It's totally my fault. I'll work all night if I have to," Kamara said, fear clouding her pale brown eyes.

"Listen," James sighed. He laced his fingers behind his neck contemplatively. "If it was a personal matter, you should have told me. I'm not a complete asshole."

Hmm, that's debatable. Gemma slid farther down her seat, nearly slipping under the table. Suddenly the hot pink camisole she'd borrowed from Dana seemed like a *really* bad wardrobe choice.

"Hey, you!" James boomed, pointing at Gemma.

Damn you, pink camisole!

"Where's Mikayla?" he asked.

Gemma gave a meek shrug.

"Then you have to help," he ordered, tugging vigorously at a gold chain around his neck. His lizard-eyes shifted from Gemma to Kamara. "We're way behind schedule and no one's called to confirm travel with the guests."

James muttered something inaudible under his breath and glanced at his watch. "I'm late for a conference call," he whined, stomping out of the room.

"That was a nightmare," Kamara groaned, fanning her face with the computer printout in her left hand. "Will you call our show guests while I go kill myself?"

Gemma smiled, assuming that Kamara was kidding.

"It's not hard, but I have so much other stuff to do," Kamara whimpered and rolled her neck painfully. "Just make sure our guests know their flight and car info. The travel department usually does it, but I don't trust them today. Did you see the brownies that stoner guy Keith brought in this morning? I'm guessing they're not filled with chocolate chips…"

"I'd love to help," Gemma nodded enthusiastically. She pushed aside the stack of flyers and followed Kamara to the phone at Bobby's desk.

"I'll do the first one," Kamara said, cradling the phone between her ear and shoulder as she flipped through a stapled stack of itineraries. "Just pretend you're a telemarketer." She dialed the ex-prostitute from Houston's phone number and ran through her travel plans in less than two minutes. "See?" she said, hanging up the phone. "Easy peasy."

"It's weird," Gemma noticed, flipping through the itineraries. "I did all that Internet research, but talking to these people on the phone is going to make them seem, like, *real.*"

Deep.

Gemma blushed, realizing that no one gave a shit about her existential awakening. Once Kamara left, Gemma snatched up the phone in a burst of self-confidence and dialed the first number. Having the PA room to herself helped some. With any luck she'd finish the calls sans audience.

"Hullo?" a little boy's voice screeched through the receiver.

Gemma looked down at the itinerary. This must be Lee, Mr. and Mrs. Cronin's eight-year-old son. The Cronin's were the ones whose daughter had been killed by her pimp. *This ought to be a fun conversation.* "Is your mommy there?"

"Uh-huh," he said. The lollypop suckfest coming from his end of the phone nearly deafened her.

"Can I talk to her?" Gemma prodded.

The phone clunked to the floor. "Hello?" Mrs. Cronin said a moment later.

Gemma's knuckles turned white from strangling the phone. "Hi…Uh, hi Mrs. Cronin," she sputtered. "I'm Gemma Winters. From *Back Talk with Kate Morgan?*"

"Hi Gemma!" the woman chirped. "Nice of you to call! How's the Big Apple?"

"Fine," Gemma replied, confused. What was up with Mrs. Cronin? Gemma hadn't expected her to sound so... chipper. A pimp had murdered her daughter, after all. Wasn't she, like, completely devastated?

Gemma soon found out—and then some. They were on the phone for forty-five minutes, and by the end she knew everything but Mrs. Cronin's bra size.

Finally, Gemma hung up the phone and looked down at the itineraries. She leafed through the pages, noticing an unfamiliar buzz surging through her body. She felt high. Not pot high—Gemma was way too neurotic for that—but more like a power high. Mrs. Cronin, who was probably fifty, treated Gemma like a respected figure of authority. How cool is *that*?

She put the phone to her swollen head and sailed through the next call to an aptly named therapist, Dr. Wellman. Gemma was pretty damn good at this, if she did say so herself. But then she paused, puffing out her cheeks as she wrapped the phone cord around her pinky finger. The next call might be tricky. She picked up the article on Crystal Bloom, lazily flipping through it. Suddenly her eyes started to spasm. Crystal Bloom... Was it just Gemma's neurotic paranoia, or did that name sound *really* familiar?

Gemma gasped, smacking her pudgy hand against her mouth as her little brain spun around like a hamster wheel. Had those skanky twins pilfered *her* article? Un-*fucking*-believable. It made sense, though. How else could they have found it when they'd been out with Timothy all day? She jumped out of her swivel chair like her itchy wool pants were on fire. Some kind of Nancy Drew bug had crawled up her ass and she was desperate to share her discovery.

Share it with whom? The we-give-a-shit-about-your-pathetic-conspiracy-theories police? They had pretty selective hours.

Gemma's nostrils flared to the size of wasabi peas as she took a deep breath. She needed to chill. Burying the twins sounded heavenly, but it would have to wait. Mr. Psycho Sweat Stains needed her to confirm travel, and she still hadn't called Crystal. Gulp. Setting aside her paranoia, Gemma sat in her chair and picked up the phone, slowly dialing Crystal Bloom's cell phone number.

A babyish voice answered the phone on the fourth ring.

"Crystal?" Gemma asked timidly.

"Who's this?" She sounded like a bulldog on helium.

"Hey, I'm Gemma. I work with Carla at *Back Talk with Kate Morgan.*" She wanted to put Crystal at ease, but her soothing voice had a certain cult-like urgency.

"When do I gets my cash?" Crystal asked in urban-white-girl slang.

Gemma shrugged. "Didn't you work that out with Carla?"

"Yeah," Crystal barked. "But y'all better make sure it's greenbacks. I can't be cashin' no checks."

"Cash, sure," Gemma agreed. She looked down at the itinerary. This girl was only *thirteen?*

"So, are you ... okay?" Gemma winced. She hated being asked that.

"Yeah, whatever," Crystal yawned.

"So, I'm supposed to make sure you have your travel info." Gemma paused to read the sheet in front of her. "We've got you at the W Hotel on Tuesday night with a car service picking you up Wednesday morning at nine."

"Uh-huh."

Sound *more* bored.

Gemma ripped the edge off the itinerary, tearing it into tiny bits. The awkward silence was going to give her an ulcer. She pressed the receiver to her ear, focusing on the faint music and poppidy popping sounds in the background.

"What's that racket?"

"Racket?" Crystal laughed critically. "What'd you say?"

"Oh god," Gemma moaned, humiliated almost to the point of heart failure. "Did I just say that? I'm only sixteen. I shouldn't even *know* that word. Seriously, though," she giggled, "what's popping?"

"It's fucking popcorn," Crystal barked, making it sound like the eighth deadly sin. "I'm at the movies—if that's *ooo-kaay.*"

Yup, definitely thirteen.

"What movie?" Gemma asked, drumming her foot restlessly against the floor. She *so* wanted to get off the phone but she couldn't shut up. Nervous habit.

"Huh?" Crystal said. She sounded taken aback. "Some foreign movie at this revival theater. I think it's called *Amelie*, or something."

Well hot damn. *Amelie* was one of Gemma's favorite films. Seriously, who doesn't love an adorably neurotic

French chick with kooky friends and a penchant for fairy-tales? "It's really good. I think you'll like it."

"One of my regulars said that, too."

"Oh." For a second Gemma had forgotten about the fact that Crystal had "regulars." "Well, I should get back to work."

"What's your name, again?" Crystal asked. Her voice was quiet but pleading.

"Gemma."

"I don't know if I can go on TV," Crystal blurted out. She sounded scared. It didn't take a genius to see that there was a lot of complicated shit in her life, and going on TV might just make it worse. "I need the cash, but I dunno if I can risk being seen."

"What?" Gemma choked. She swallowed hard, trying to keep her Cheerios down. This was bad. *Very* bad. "Is somebody trying to talk you out of doing the show?"

Gemma paused and took a deep breath, realizing the urgency in her voice must be scaring the crap out of Crystal. "I don't blame you. I can't imagine what you're going through." Her head was throbbing and she had no idea how to talk a hooker off the proverbial ledge.

"Maybe telling your story would be therapeutic?" she finally suggested.

"Hhh," Crystal breathed heavily. "I gotta go." There was a minute of silence so painful it shaved years off Gemma's life.

"Let me give you my cell number," Gemma begged, rattling off the digits. "Call me whenever you want."

"Fine," Crystal mumbled. The phone went dead.

"Surprise, surprise!" Nick purred as the elevator doors swung open. He had on gray khakis and a crisp white button-down with a stormy, sea-green tie that looked dyed to match his eyes.

Did he ever *not* look like a Tommy Hilfiger model?

Gemma walked into the elevator, tugging at her pink camisole to amp up the cleavage factor. She was still bugging out about Crystal, but she easily managed a coy smile and fluttery wave.

Funny how a hot guy can melt your troubles away.

Gemma leaned against the wall just two inches from Nick. Bold move considering the elevator was otherwise empty. She looked down, blinking at the gold-and-sapphire boulder on Nick's pinky finger. It was nice, in a Tony-Soprano-for-Jostens kind of way.

"It's my frat ring," he said, bringing his knuckles to Gemma's face for inspection.

If she'd known how to compliment a man's ring she would have, but pretty and sparkly hardly seemed like masculine adjectives. Her flustered smile kind of said it all. Muzak filled the air and Nick laughed. Gemma joined in when she realized it was a Michael Boltonesque version of "Hot in Herre." As far as she was concerned, it definitely was.

"I can't wait till the weekend," Gemma sighed, trying to make conversation. She rolled her eyes, suddenly reminded of the "I carried a watermelon" quote from *Dirty Dancing*.

"Big date?" Nick asked, raising his eyebrow playfully.

"No," Gemma giggled. But she was flattered that he would ask.

"I'm surprised, but glad," he whispered, leaning closer. "Hey, if you're free Saturday, why don't you come to a party at my place?"

The elevator doors opened onto the lobby but Gemma was frozen. Ever since she'd met Nick, she'd wanted him to ask her out, but dreaming about it and having it actually happen were two totally different things. She smiled nervously, searching for meaning in Nick's big, green eyes. He *was* asking her out, right? This was all so new to her and she couldn't tell if party meant *Party!* or party-in-my-pants.

"Bring your friends," Nick added, correctly interpreting her fear-struck expression. He laced his fingers through Gemma's and gently pulled her off the elevator. "What were their names again? Asia and Dana?"

"*America* and Dana," Gemma laughed. Aw, he was trying to be cute. "We'd love to come!"

Never mind that they're not on speaking terms.

"Cool," Nick smiled, pulling a business card out of his wallet and jotting down his Williamsburg address.

Gemma crinkled her eyebrows, looking back and forth between the address and Nick. Dana had described Williamsburg as the pencil-jeans-wearing, Dumpster-diving, hipster capital of the world. It was hard to picture Nick like that.

"See you then," Gemma smiled, pushing through the revolving doors and heading toward the subway. She bought a salty pretzel from a street vendor and walked up along Central Park West. She was ecstatic. The guy of her dreams had just invited her to a party. All she had to do now was figure out what to wear.

FIFTEEN

"Hello?" Gemma mumbled, blearily answering her phone from sleepyland. She rubbed her eyes and looked down at her bedside table. 3:30 a.m.

"You said I could call if I needed to."

Huh? It sounded like Gemma's little sister, but Gemma didn't *have* a little sister.

"What's wrong?" Gemma asked. She'd play along till she could assess the situation.

"You were right about people not wanting me to go on TV."

Crystal! Good, she wanted to talk. Gemma scrambled out of bed and turned the lights on. "I'm glad you called, Crystal. Where are you?"

Crystal's silence was understandable. She probably didn't trust anyone farther than she could throw them. Gemma waited patiently, listening to Crystal's shaky breath.

"Do you want to meet me for coffee?" Gemma asked softly. "I'll buy you a burger or something if you want."

Crystal hesitated for another moment then mumbled, "Fine."

Good. Progress. "Where do you want to go? Should I meet you in your neighborhood?"

Gemma? In the seedy outskirts of Queens? Perish the thought.

"No," Crystal quickly jumped in. "I gotta get out of here. I'll come to you."

Gemma shook two packets of Splenda into her coffee and stirred it with a bent spoon. The Three Star Diner was totally dead and she felt about as happy to be there as the hunchback waitress who'd seated her. Yawning for the hundredth time, Gemma looked down at the digital clock on her cell phone. Nearly four a.m. Crystal Bloom would be there any minute now. She nervously sipped her lukewarm coffee, trying not to notice the creepy busboy ogling her from behind the counter.

Crystal was easy to spot when she drifted in ten minutes later—the wife-beater and tiny denim Band-Aid of a skirt were hard to miss. The lacy red thong peeking up around her waist was a nice touch, too. Gemma watched in awed

fascination as the no-more-than-five-foot-two pigtailed brunette wandered toward her booth. Her freckled face was
caked with makeup, and too many trips to the tanning salon
had given her an Oompa-Loompa-ish glow. Tanning was a
trick of the trade—it covered bruises quite effectively—but
Gemma didn't know that.

Crystal dropped her MP3 player into the side pocket of
her black-and-pink-heart-printed LeSportsac overnighter
and sat across from Gemma. This was too surreal. Gemma
was in a crappy Manhattan diner at four in the morning,
about to have coffee with a thirteen-year-old hooker. Her
parents *definitely* didn't need to hear about *this*.

"So are you going to buy me a burger or what?" Crystal
asked in her gruff, babyish voice. She whistled for a menu
and flipped through it lazily.

Gemma nodded. "Just don't go crazy. I'm not getting
paid this summer."

"Huh?" Crystal gaped, looking up from the burger section.

"It's an internship," Gemma explained lamely. Suddenly
she wasn't sure Crystal knew what an internship was. "You
know, so I can learn—"

"'Scuse me?" Crystal bellowed. "I'm not a *re*tard."

"Sorry," Gemma mumbled. *Way to go, fuckwad.*

Crystal closed her menu and snapped for the disgrun-
tled waitress. "Veggie burger and a salad. No fries."

"Healthy," Gemma observed. She could never resist
French fries.

"I'm a vegetarian," Crystal replied defensively. "My family drove cross-country when I was, like, eight and we passed a slaughterhouse. It was *so* rank. When my parents told me what they did inside, I was like '*hell* no.' I never ate meat since."

Gemma smiled and nodded, suddenly feeling guilty about meatloaf Mondays at the Winters household. She sat in silence for a minute, watching Crystal blow big purple Bubble Yum bubbles while she nervously drummed her acrylic nails against the table to the Spanish power ballad coming from the kitchen.

"Do you miss it?" Gemma finally asked. "Family, not meat."

Crystal half-smiled at Gemma's lame joke and poured five packets of sugar onto the table. With her Pepto-pink pinky she swirled it around in a haphazard curly cue pattern. "I miss my dad, I guess."

"Do you ever call home?" Gemma prodded. She was really getting the nosy and inquisitive New Yorker thing down. "You know, just to let him know you're all right?"

"My dad's dead, okay?" Crystal hissed. The sugar jumped an inch as she pounded her fist angrily against the table.

Strike two for fuckwad. But how was Gemma supposed to know? Dana would have been good in this situation, having a dead dad and all. Gemma's nuclear family hardly gave her license to dispense grief counseling. She quietly sipped her coffee, searching for something, *anything*, to say when the waitress arrived with Crystal's burger. She plopped it down on top of the sugar masterpiece and refilled Gemma's coffee.

Crystal scooped the salad greens onto her burger and squeezed yellow mustard on the bun. "You want to hear my story, don't you?" Crystal said, rolling her eyes. She picked up her mushy veggie burger, took a huge bite and said, "My dad died when I was eleven. Then Mom and I moved from Boulder to Scarsdale, New York. She got remarried right away and as soon as they were back from the honeymoon my new stepdad raped me."

Whoa! Gemma coughed violently.

Crystal smirked at Gemma's squeamishness and continued. "It happened almost every night for a year. I couldn't sleep. I couldn't eat. I begged him to stop, but—" Crystal paused for another bite like she was talking about a coffee stain. The truth was, she'd told her story a million times and there were girls on the street who'd been through a lot worse. "One day my friend Megan told me her brother was doing the same shit to her and she was gonna run away. I don't know why, but that gave me the balls to finally tell my mom."

"What did she say?" Gemma asked, wide eyed.

"She didn't believe me," Crystal shrugged, wiping mustard off her dimpled chin. "She took my stepdad's side. What a bitch, right?" she added, her mousy voice laden with sarcasm.

Gemma was horrified. "Why didn't you report your stepfather to the police?"

"If my own *mother* didn't believe me, who would?"

"Uh, the *police*," Gemma said, a little glibber than she'd meant to. "They're required to look into those kinds of accusations. That's what social workers are for."

Crystal shrugged like it didn't matter so Gemma dropped it.

"Do you have a pimp?" she asked. Morbid curiosity was getting the better of her and she kept picturing Crystal with some tall skinny dude in plaid bell-bottoms and a feather in his hat. "Never mind," she quickly added, detecting a sudden chill in the air.

"Don't sweat it," Crystal said, smirking at her burger. The mother of all burps came out of her small, heart-shaped mouth and she smiled satisfactorily. "His name's Kenny. He screens guys and sends 'em to this park a couple of us girls hang out at." She paused to pop the last bite of burger into her mouth then crumpled her napkin on the empty plate. "Without Kenny I'd be blowing pedophiles in an alley—or dead."

Or getting your life back together, Gemma remarked in the comfort of her own head. She was a chicken shit, but what do you say to the girl who's been molested by her stepfather, beaten by her pimp, and makes sixty bucks a pop to service random men?

"You don't just do hooker stuff all day though, right?" Gemma finally asked/accused. Hey, it was practically five a.m.—she was tired. "I mean, don't you want to *be* something when you grow up?"

Crystal ignored her, reapplying her pearly pink Wet n Wild lipstick. Finally she reached into her bag and pulled out a tattered black case. Inside was a vintage-looking thirty-five millimeter Nikon camera. She handed it gingerly to Gemma. "It was my dad's."

"Cool," Gemma commented. She didn't know jack about cameras, but it looked like a nice one.

Crystal took it back and quickly snapped a picture of Gemma. "I used to want to be a photographer. I could go around the world and shoot for—what's that one magazine called? The one with all the pictures?"

"*National Geographic*?" Gemma suggested.

"Yeah. That'd be phat." Crystal clicked several photos of the waitress while she tallied up her receipts at the counter. "I take all kinds of pictures of buildings and the girls on the street. South Street Seaport's a chill place to shoot. There's so many tourists there I can, like, disappear."

Crystal lowered her head and examined the Nikon's rusty setting options. All of a sudden she actually looked thirteen and not just like some badass munchkin street hustler. Kind of refreshing.

"I love photography," Gemma said supportively. "You know you can go to college for that?"

"Yeah right. Like *I'm* going to college," Crystal scoffed. "I dropped out of eighth grade." She breathed delicately on the camera's lens and cleaned it with a silk cloth.

"Maybe Kate Morgan can help you," Gemma suggested casually.

Not casually enough. Crystal rolled her eyes heavily, tugging at her pigtails.

Gemma must have channeled her inner-mom for that one. She zipped her mouth shut theatrically and stared out the window, twisting her silver bracelet. There were all kinds of programs out there for girls like Crystal, but if Gemma mentioned any of them she'd just sound like some preachy Brady Bunch psycho.

"You need to leave Kenny," she finally blurted. She couldn't resist. "He is exploiting you. People who love you shouldn't beat you and steal from you."

Crystal didn't argue, which Gemma took as a good sign, and then, in an instant, she started to cry. Only a little, but enough to make Gemma's heart break.

"Kenny doesn't know about me going on TV," Crystal said softly. "He found out about the newspaper article, though. The reporter guy paid me and my friend Desiree two hundred bucks to talk to him, and when Kenny found out … ," she paused to wipe a few tears from her cheek with Gemma's clean napkin. "When he found out he broke Desiree's arm. She ran away and the fuzz got her. I heard she's in juvy now." She lifted up her white wife-beater, revealing a round, reddish scab above her belly button. "This is all I got."

"Oh my god, is that a *cigar* burn?" Gemma winced. "Crystal, I'm so sorry. Hey, do you need a place to stay tonight?"

Crystal quickly shook her head and pulled a black cashmere cardigan out of her bag. "I can't. Kenny's probably shitting bricks 'cuz I haven't checked in yet." She pulled her cell phone out, too, and checked it for messages. Then she carefully put her camera back in its case and back into her bag.

Gemma took fifteen dollars out of her Kate Spade wallet and placed it on the table underneath Crystal's empty plate and scooted out of the booth. "Hey," she said brightly— they needed a subject change, stat. "Did you like *Amelie*?"

For the first time all night, a sweet smile spread across Crystal's lips. "It was pretty ah'right. Good thing I read fast. Subtitles are a bitch. I liked the lawn gnome."

Gemma laughed in agreement. She pushed through the heavy glass door and out onto Eighty-Sixth Street where the electric blue sky reflected off cars and buildings. It had to be almost six in the morning. Gemma cringed, realizing she had to be at work in three hours.

That should be fun.

"Sorry I kept you out so late," Crystal yawned, noticing the pained expression on Gemma's face. She pulled her cardigan tightly around her small shoulders and waved. "Good night." She flashed a weak smile and walked east toward the park.

Gemma giggled, noticing Crystal's lime green leather-with-gold-piping platform heels. She stood there for a second, watching Crystal walk away.

"Good *morning*," Gemma whimpered quietly. She looked at Crystal for another second, then headed south down Columbus toward home.

SIXTEEN

No amount of coffee was going to do the trick, not even Gemma's double espresso Frappuccino from Starbucks, unless "the trick" was a heart palpitation and the shakes. She breathed heavily, whizzing down the *Back Talk* corridor in a brand-new floral tank dress. *Must find Carla, must find Carla*, Gemma chanted maniacally. She snapped her fingers with urgency as she poked her head into every room, finally slamming into Carla in the reception area.

"Sorry," Gemma apologized, resting her hand on Carla's lavender sweater-set to steady herself. "I'm totally hyper. But thank god I found you. Something crazy happened last night."

Carla fidgeted uncomfortably, her eyes darting around the room. Nobody gave a shit about interns and she was no exception.

"It's about Crystal," Gemma continued, following Carla down the hall to her office. "She sounded super nervous when I called with her itinerary yesterday so I gave her my cell number. You know, just in case she needed to talk?"

"That was brave," Carla smirked, oozing insincerity. "I loathe giving out my home number to guests. I'm not a fucking babysitter."

Clearly.

Gemma let out a Dr. Evil-ish chuckle, creeping out both Carla and herself. No more espresso for this little piggy. "Crystal ended up calling me late last night," Gemma explained. "She was having second thoughts about doing the show so I met up with her."

Carla's face turned a dismal shade of I-just-threw-up-in-my-mouth gray as she grabbed Gemma's shoulders tightly. "Is she still going to do the show?"

"Probably?" Gemma ventured halfheartedly.

"I guess her pimp found out about the article and, like, burnt her with a cigar." Gemma shuddered just thinking about it. "She's freaked out. But I was thinking, can't Kate Morgan do something to help her? Like, put her in protective custody or whatever?"

"Uh-huh," Carla replied distractedly. She sped down the hallway, pulling Gemma along with her. "You've got to tell James about this, but listen..." There was concern in her voice as she stopped to look Gemma in the eyes. "Don't make it sound *too* severe or I'll have to scrape his ass off the ceiling."

Gemma gulped. *I'm so fired.* She clutched the doorframe tightly for safety as Carla dragged her into James's office. His cheap, Marlboro Man/cotton candy cologne nearly made her gag as she and Carla stood there, waiting for James to get off the phone. She could tell by his inflection that it was a personal call, which wasn't a big surprise.

Everyone scams free phone calls at work. It's the American way.

"What's the weather like?" James murmured into the receiver.

Carla rolled her eyes and finally rapped her knuckles on the door. *It's important*, she mouthed. James nodded and winked, shifting languidly in his chair. Once he'd hung up, he propped his elbows on the desk and rested his chin on his fists expectantly.

"Gemma saw Crystal last night," Carla sighed accusingly. "She might back out of the show."

What happened to *not too severe?*

"Son of a ..." James crumpled in his chair dramatically. Mr. Sleazy James Bond didn't look so hot. "This can't be happening to me."

Gemma waited until the silence was too excruciating to bear, then said, "It might not be totally hopeless." Her petrified smile was less than convincing. "Well, Crystal and I talked for hours ..." Gemma drifted off, biting her lip. Talk Show 101: a great guest is a talkative guest. If Crystal dropped out, they'd be losing a goldmine—maybe even a Daytime Emmy nomination. Seriously, who'd tune in to watch some toothless redneck grunting like a caveman? *Exactly.* So losing Crystal would be major salt in the wound.

"What did she say?" James asked desperately. "What did you tell her? She must want something. Anonymity? We can put her in silhouette. Or is it money? Does she want more money? Talk to me, talk to me!"

Gemma took a deep breath and tried to process the barrage of questions being hurled at her. She was starting to freak out. Each breath became shorter and quicker and suddenly Gemma felt a panic attack coming on. Poor Gemma. If she was going to hyperventilate every time things got tense, TV *might* not be the place for her. She shut her eyes tight and tried to remember a specific memory from her conversation with Crystal.

"She wants to be a photographer," Gemma blurted out. "She's got this really old Nikon camera, but she doesn't have any faith in herself. Maybe we could send her to a special school or, like, a halfway house."

James clasped his index fingers together and tapped his chin thoughtfully. He pushed himself out of his swivel chair and paced back and forth in his signature retired-glam-rocker jeans. Gemma was a little freaked out by the far-off glint in his eye—think Jack Nicholson in *The Shining*—but the fact that he was humming the *Jeopardy!* theme kind of balanced it out. He looked like some kind of mad genius. Or better yet, a talk show savant.

"Carla!" James screamed, scaring the crap out of both girls. "Call Judy over at that clinic. You know, the one from the homeless show? See what she can do. Have Kamara call every boarding school, mentoring program, and juvy facility in the tri-state area. And Gemma, grab a seat. You're going to repeat your conversation with Crystal, word for word."

Carla was out of the room in a flash, and Gemma just stood there, gaping at James. He scrambled to his desk and clicked around frantically to open a new Word document on his Mac. With fingers hovering over the keyboard, he stared at Gemma, waiting for her to relay the previous night's events. It felt like the interrogation room in *Law & Order*. James played a schizo version of good-cop bad-cop while madly typing away, urging Gemma to elaborate and deconstruct her little heart out. Thank god she hadn't slept or the story might not have been as fresh in her mind. She speedily tapped her foot against the gray carpet, regurgitating every detail that came to her, from the lecherous busboy to the 15 percent tip she'd left the hunchback waitress. Even when James exploded at her for taking his show, *his baby*, into her own hands, she managed to stay calm and on track. She kicked ass.

Who's the talk show savant now?

SEVENTEEN

"Are you nervous?"

Gemma rolled her eyes. Dana had asked her that, like, ten million times already.

The two of them were dressed to kill—or at least to induce shock—and heading across the Williamsburg Bridge to Nick's party. So yes, it was safe to say that Gemma was freaking out. She couldn't focus on anything else. Not browsing makeup at Sephora, or the Matt Damon blockbuster at the IMAX, or even the fact that Dana and America still weren't on speaking terms, which was racking her with guilt, by the way. Three days of silence and her stupid roommates *still* hadn't worked things out. America and

Danny were obviously into each other but Dana refused to see it. She was one stubborn bitch when she had a grudge.

"I'm *not* nervous," Gemma grumped. She looked out the cab window, focusing on Manhattan as it grew smaller and smaller in the distance. Her silk maroon wrap top blew open slightly and she pulled it tight across her chest, letting out a frustrated sigh. The slippery top was really starting to piss her off, but she tried to chill out. Compared to the rest of the bullshit unraveling in her brain, a wrap top was minor pittance. First of all, she still couldn't decide if this was a date or a pity invite; and secondly, did Nick even know she was just sixteen? The underage thing might be a turnoff for some guys.

"You'll be fine!" Dana reassured, massaging Gemma's shoulders like Rocky on fight night. "And *I'll* be there to protect you."

Gemma winced at Dana's implication that she was a better friend. Seriously, these if-you-come-to-the-party-I'll-kill-you looks Dana had been shooting America would have scared Paris Hilton away.

"We're gonna have a great time. And either way," Dana added, pulling a crisp twenty out of her ivory Dolce Vita ankle boot, "We're here. So suck it up and deal."

The cab pulled to a halt and Gemma slid out. God, she was a nervous wreck. She clung to a lamppost to steady herself and blushed with embarrassment as a girl in a belted gray T-shirt dress breezed past. Dana was right, Williamsburg was painfully hip and Gemma *so* did not fit in.

"This way," Dana nodded. She took Gemma's hand supportively and skipped down the sidewalk after a group of twenty-somethings carrying beer and wine.

"You're like a *narc* dog," Gemma quipped.

"Everyone's got a talent," Dana shrugged, quickly crossing the street toward a ramshackle building. One of the twenty-somethings held the heavy metal door open for them and Dana smiled gratefully, mouthing *He's hot!* to Gemma.

They could hear indie pop from the entryway and it only got louder as the girls clomped up to the fifth floor. Gemma heaved a dizzy sigh as she neared the third floor. Regular exercise had become a distant memory. She smirked, noticing a clump of stickers along the wall, and one in particular that said, *Potatoriot.com: 'cuz brain-eating zombies roll like that.*

"Wow, not bad," Dana screamed over the music. She pushed her way through Nick's front hall, nodding approvingly at the space. See, some Manhattanites have a thing against Brooklyn—it's like a battle of the boroughs—but Dana had to admit the converted warehouse had gorgeously high ceilings and tons of space. The overall décor was a little Pier One for her taste, but she'd yet to meet a straight guy with style.

Gemma clung to the back of Dana's vintage crocheted mini-dress as they waded through the living room. Her eyes darted around and around, scanning desperately for a familiar face. There had to be a hundred people crammed in there, and if Gemma didn't spot someone soon she was afraid Dana would think she didn't have any friends. She was considering slipping someone a twenty to *pretend* to be her friend, when—

"Gemma!" Melissa sang, tapping Gemma on the shoulder.

Thank god. Gemma gave Melissa a grateful hug and waved at Clark dancing behind her. "I'm so glad you guys are here!"

Melissa smiled, pulling Dana and Gemma into the middle of the room to dance. "This party's jumpin'," she yelled. She shook her butt in tune to an indie cover of YMCA and nodded toward a circle of people dancing in the corner. "Did you check out Sweet Valley High over there?"

Gemma danced self-consciously, following Melissa's gaze toward Anita and Maria. "Oh, *god*," she giggled, rolling her eyes. They were bumpin' and grindin' like sluts in a Kid Rock video.

"You're *kid*ding!" Dana whooped, curving her arms to the retro YMCA chant. "If I wasn't such a bitch, I'd feel totally embarrassed for them."

"Daddy must be *so* proud," Clark deadpanned, also curving his arms YMCA-style. "But check out this music! Isn't it hilarious? One of Nick's roommates is a DJ."

DJ? Gemma tensed immediately at the word. She flashed Dana a concerned look, and both girls looked around the room. It probably wasn't Dana's DJ but they had to be sure. Finally Dana spotted the short, beefy Japanese DJ and sighed with relief. He was cute but he wasn't her guy. She flashed a mopey smile and started dancing again.

"And," Melissa added quietly, "GraphNix is looking mighty fine tonight. Hook it *up*, girl!"

Gemma blushed. Melissa better not have blabbed to anyone that she was crushing on Nick Daltrey. How humiliating would that be? She pulled the subtle I'm-scratching-my-shoulder-with-my-chin maneuver and scanned the room for Nick. Bingo. She finally spotted him, in all his splendor, leaning against the wall talking to a hot blonde chick. Of *course* he was talking to a hottie.

"It's never going to happen," Gemma sighed.

"Not if you act like *that*," Dana accused, swatting her hand in Gemma's general direction. "Somewhere in that frizzy mop, you know you're cute, so freakin' act like it already!"

"Seriously," Clark added. "*I* act like a bigger diva than you."

"You *are* a bigger diva than me," Gemma huffed. Was this an intervention or something?

"You're into movies, right?" Melissa asked, switching gears. "Pretend you're someone else. Someone ballsy, like ... Julia Roberts in *Pretty Woman*."

"Let's see," Gemma pondered sarcastically, tapping her finger against her lower lip. "Because I'm not a *hooker*?"

Without explanation, Clark's eyes bulged and he shoved Gemma backwards. *What the fuck?* She wobbled frantically, almost falling flat on her ass when suddenly Nick appeared.

What are the chances?

"Whoa, little lady!" he crooned, imitating John Wayne. "You all right?" He chivalrously took Gemma's arm to steady her. Damn, he looked good—as usual. And as usual, Gemma's legs turned to jelly when she looked into his sparkly green eyes.

"Sorry," she giggled, tugging at her top. "I guess I lost my balance." She thought about bolting, but she was trying to *lose* her socially awkward reputation, not enhance it. That, and if she ran she'd never hear the end of it from her eavesdropping entourage.

"You look great, Gem," Nick murmured with a lazy smile. "I'm glad you came."

Swoon. "You've got a great apartment," Gemma commented lamely. At least she wasn't drooling on him. "How many roommates do you have?"

Nick paused to smile at a group of girls dancing nearby. "There're four of us. It's sorta like a dorm, but it's mad cheap. We've been talking about throwing a party for a while, but I guess it took my birthday to make it happen."

Gemma's eyes brightened. "It's your birthday?"

Nick shrugged, smiling sheepishly.

"I wish I'd known," she frowned. "I would have brought you something."

Nick squeezed Gemma's hand playfully. "Oh yeah?" he winked. "A present? Maybe we can work something out later…"

Gemma smiled awkwardly, not sure if this was a sleazy come-on or a genuine request for a belated birthday gift.

Be *more* naïve.

"I think we've got an audience," Nick added, clearing his throat.

Looking over her shoulder at her gawking friends, Gemma gasped with embarrassment. God, couldn't her friends just eavesdrop like normal people? She shot them individual death stares and turned back to Nick, attempting a breezy smile. "Sorry about that. They're my personal studio audience. So ..." she took a deep breath to psych herself up. "Do you want to give me a tour?" She winked, letting a playful smile linger on her lips.

Mee-*yow*.

Nick grinned approvingly, letting his hand drift around Gemma's waist as he guided her through the crowd. The music had switched to old school hip-hop and Gemma bobbed her head from side to side, taking way too much pleasure in the fact that her dream guy was parading her around. He pushed through a swinging door and into a beer-can-and-pretzel-crumb-filled kitchen. Sweeping aside an empty cup with his K-Swiss sneaker, Nick fanned his arms out in a grand, Vanna White gesture.

"Do you cook?" Gemma asked, eyeing an expensive KitchenAid mixer filled with Cheetos.

"Does Kraft Mac & Cheese count? J.K." he laughed.

J.K.? Is this an I.M.?

"My roommate Marco is a pastry chef," Nick explained. "But I have a few culinary tricks up my sleeve ... for special occasions."

Gemma blushed.

Nick grabbed her hand again and led her out of the kitchen and down an unlit hallway. Pointing to the first door on the right, he said, "This is Ronnie's room. He's also studying graphic design at NYU. He's only got a year left, though—bastard. And next is Kenji's room. You probably saw him in the living room at the turntables. He's a killer DJ. On the left is the bathroom. You can check that out when nature calls. And that's Marco's room. And last but not least ..." He pointed at a door covered in *Simpsons* stickers. "My room."

Gemma smiled casually, trying not to have a seizure. She watched Nick turn the doorknob and followed him into a pretty average *guy* room. It looked like her brother's, which was sad considering Derek was only fourteen and Nick was twenty.

"Neat," was all she could think to say about his pathetic high school basketball trophies. She walked in a little farther, finding his arsenal of colognes and grooming products much more engrossing. She picked up a tube of Ben*efit* moisturizer called *You Rebel* and stifled a giggle. Nick was a metrosexual, in the flesh! Guys like this didn't exist in Idaho.

"Glad you like it," Nick said as he leaned against his desk, fingering the largest of said trophies.

Going for flirty rather than easy, Gemma sat down on the bed ... and rippled. *A waterbed?* Nothing against waterbeds, but weren't they kind of a porn thing?

Bawm-chicka-bow-bow.

"I love that bed," Nick grinned, mistaking Gemma's perturbed stupor for appreciation. "I'm from California. It reminds me of the Pacific."

Bad Gemma! She yanked her mind out of the gutter and smiled up at Nick. Who doesn't like the ocean? "It's great," she agreed, going with the flow until she felt seasick.

Nick gave a sly smile as he watched Gemma bounce on his waterbed. "So, what do you think of *Back Talk*?" he finally asked. "This is my second summer interning and I think they're gonna put me on staff when I graduate in a couple years." He paused, fixing his gaze on Gemma. "It looks like you're having fun, too. I've had my eye on you."

Nick's eye on me? Gemma nearly fell off the bed. "It's a blast," she gushed. "I love the lingo. Bumps, SOT, MOS, suckbacks … it's like a different language."

"I don't know half of what you just said and I've been working there for two years," Nick laughed.

"Maybe I'll teach you," Gemma said in a gravelly, lounge singer voice.

"Sounds good."

Nick pushed himself off the desk and sauntered over to Gemma, trying not to disturb the waves as he sat next to her. Fat chance. The mattress rippled and they both giggled a little. Then, with a well-manicured hand, Nick caressed Gemma's face and pressed his lips hard against hers. He tasted like chips and beer but Gemma overlooked it, reminding herself that this was a major fantasy fulfilled. She opened her mouth tentatively as Nick wrapped his arms around her back, massaging it lightly as his kisses gradually became more urgent. Gemma kissed back, eager to match his intensity, but hot n' heavy wasn't in her resume. What if she messed up?

Not like he'd notice.

Nick slipped his hands under Gemma's top, tugging at her bra clasp with unparalleled determination. The bra wouldn't budge, and after a few unsuccessful attempts he yanked it down around her waist. Jackpot. He groaned appreciatively, his hands making their way to the front of her chest like vultures. Before she could stop herself Gemma yelped, pushing Nick off of her.

"It's cool," Nick whispered, softly brushing hair away from Gemma's face. "Don't worry. I'll be back in a minute, okay, beautiful?" He let out a tortured sigh and sauntered out of his room, shutting the door behind him.

What is my problem? Gemma silently chastised. For a moment she just sat there, dizzily struggling to catch her breath. This *was* what she'd wanted, right? Suddenly she couldn't remember. She pulled her bra straps over her shoulders and smoothed down her unkempt hair. Nick obviously liked her, which was reassuring, but why did he have to be so aggressive? Gemma shrugged her shoulders up and down to relax. Nick wasn't treating her like a kid so she better stop acting like one.

"You okay?" he asked softly, reappearing in the doorway with a six-pack of Coors Light. He set the beer down on the desk and dimmed the wall light. "Have a beer."

Gemma accepted the can with a weak nod and tapped the lid before opening it. *Warm beer*, she smiled wryly. At least it helped settle her nerves.

"Where were we?" Nick asked, tousling his silky blonde hair and joining Gemma on the bed. "I really feel like I can be myself around you," he murmured, kissing her shoulder, her neck, and then her lips. He untied her wrap top and Gemma's heart raced as maroon silk crumpled in a heap around her waist. A lecherous smile curled on Nick's lips as he continued to kiss her hungrily, moaning the occasional "*oh baby.*" Gemma gulped. She couldn't catch her breath. Everything was happening so fast, but she was too flustered to protest. In an instant the kissing was over and Nick straddled Gemma. She tried to roll out from under him but on the waterbed it was like swimming through molasses.

"Stop!" she finally screamed at the sound of Nick's Levis unzipping. "What are you doing?"

In typical caveman fashion, Nick completely ignored her, murmuring, "Your skin is so soft," and "That feels good." Gemma squeezed her eyes shut and fought frantically to push her dream guy off of her, but in one swift motion he pinned her wrists over her head making it nearly impossible to move. She wriggled and writhed under Nick's heavy frame, vaguely recognizing an old Prince song somewhere in the distance. Suddenly it hit her. This was *really* happening, wasn't it? Gemma continued to fight, her mind filling with celluloid rape scenes and varying *no means no* scenarios. Was she going to end up another statistic like Crystal? Oh god—Crystal. Was this what it had been like the first time Crystal's stepfather came into her bedroom? Gemma thrashed her legs back and forth, whimpering, "Stop. Please stop!"

Her heart thudded like a washing machine on spin cycle.

"Hey, Nick! You in there?" a voice called from the hallway.

The groping continued but as the knocking grew louder, Nick finally eased his weight off Gemma.

Saved by the drunk-frat-boy bell.

"Just a sec." Nick reached onto the floor and grabbed a blue Lacoste polo shirt. "I'm coming," he yelled, pulling it over his head and lazily fastening his belt buckle. He turned to Gemma, finally acknowledging her tear-streaked face. "What's your problem? You're the one who asked for the tour. Remember?"

If *that* was the tour, she should ask for her money back.

Gemma clutched her top in utter horror. What was Nick insinuating? That she'd asked for it? As *if!* She wiped her eyes and looked toward the door, still waiting for Nick to answer it. Maybe later she'd deconstruct this nightmare, but right now all she wanted to do was get the *mother-F* out of there.

"Chill out, drama queen," Nick groaned, quickly losing interest. "We were just having a good time."

Ah yes, the little-known Merriam-Webster definition of "good time."

Nick grabbed a beer, pounding it in three gulps. "You're cute, but I don't think *this*," he paused briefly to point out the space between them, "is gonna work out. You're still in high school. I need someone who's a little more..." he trailed off, preoccupied with the tab on his beer can.

Gemma brushed a few tears off her cheek, suddenly feeling like an *American Idol* reject. No, even Simon Cowell wasn't *this* big a dick. She shook her head in disgust, tightening her shirt again as she squeezed past him and ran to the door. So, Nick was dumping her, before they'd even had a date, because she wouldn't let him *rape* her? Un-*fucking*-believable. She flung the door open, walking into a lanky blonde guy holding a freshly packed bong.

"Hope I'm not interrupting," bong-boy sneered.

"Get. Out. Of my way," Gemma replied through gritted teeth.

Few things on earth were going to stop her from leaving that party, and a lazy dipshit with a bong was sure as hell not one of them.

BACK TALK

"I wish you'd let me kick him in the nuts," Dana spat, pouring another shot of Jose Cuervo into her *What happens in Vegas stays in Vegas* shot glass. In recognition of Gemma's near-rape, she'd agreed to backburner the whole "feud" thing and hang out in the living room with Gemma, America, and Danny.

"No thanks," Gemma said, declining a second shot. She wasn't really in the mood for tequila—even if it was in a shot glass that said: *Your boyfriend likes me better.* "I appreciate each and every offer to beat, maim, or mutilate Nick, but I just want to drop it. I mean, he must have thought I was leading him on—maybe I'm partly to blame."

"Doubtful," Danny said from the other end of the sofa where he was massaging America's foot. "Flirting doesn't warrant date rape. He was totally out of line."

"Seriously," Dana added. "None of this 'it was my fault' bullshit, Gemma. It was his fault. Come on, *say it*."

Gemma blushed. She hated being assertive. "Okay, okay. You're right. It was *his* fault."

"I'm just sorry you had to go through that. It's not fun," America said, a little too knowingly. "You should have called the police. Or at least stolen something from his house," she added wickedly.

"America!" Gemma gasped. "I can't believe you."

Dana smiled. "I can. In fact…" She grabbed her Fendi bag off the floor and brought it to the sofa. "Tada!" she said, pulling out a bottle of Veuve Clicquot and a DVD.

"You stole champagne and a copy of *Scarface*?"

"I've never seen it," Dana shrugged, squinting as she popped the champagne cork. "To Nick," she said, taking a swig and handing the bottle to Gemma.

"To Nick," Gemma toasted. "May his balls shrivel up and fall off." She chugged a few sips, then passed the bottle to America.

After a few more derogatory toasts, Gemma was a little buzzed and feeling a lot better. She'd still have to see Nick at work all summer, which made her more than a little queasy, but she'd manage. The worst part about it was how stupid she felt. All those wasted hours spent daydreaming of Nick and his luscious lips… Now her daydreams would consist of Nick getting hit by a car; Nick being eaten alive by ants; Nick dying from food poisoning…

They were pipe dreams, but ones she could live with.

EIGHTEEN

"Conference room, everybody!" Melissa said, peeking her head into Hell on Monday morning.

"I thought staff meetings were on Tuesdays?" Gemma asked, following Melissa down the hall.

Melissa shrugged indifferently.

This sucked. Gemma was already dreading running into Nick the Dick at Tuesday's staff meeting. Now she had to see him on Monday, too? She looked down at her baggy linen jeans. They didn't exactly scream *this is what you're missing*, but it was only Monday. Nobody strategizes their *Monday* outfit. She quickly reapplied the Stila lip shimmer she'd purchased at Sephora and ducked into the conference room.

With a seat in the corner and minimal body movement, she'd be fine.

"I think someone got fired," Carla whispered to Val.

Gemma took a seat nearby and craned her neck to hear. This should be good. Carla had uncanny ESP that she attributed to her love of astrology. She was always predicting random crap like who'd get kicked off *Survivor* or how so-and-so was a bitch because she was a Scorpio. It was no surprise that she had a theory about this, too.

"Mercury is in retrograde," Carla explained. "We all know what *that* means."

Uh, sure we do.

"Okay, people." Penelope O'Shea marched into the room, a haggard, doleful look on her pale face. She took her usual seat and surveyed the room, making sure all bigwigs were accounted for.

Not that he was a bigwig, but Gemma happily confirmed Nick's absence.

Ms. O'Shea tapped her bejeweled fingers on the table and stood slowly. "Bad news. We've had to let James Finch go." She waited patiently for the whispers and gasps to subside. "I know, I know. We're all upset, but we've still got a show to run. I'm going to need cooperation here, people. I'm handing James's prostitution show over to Timothy and I'm making a few other switches. Producers: we'll meet in my office in one hour. Everyone get back to work."

Gemma sat there bewildered while the rest of the staff nodded, whispering scandalously as they exited the conference room. That was it? James was fired with no explanation? And his show was being passed over to *Timothy*? How unfair. James was, like, obsessed with that prostitution show. Gemma bit her lip, suddenly afraid she'd be pulled from the prostitution show, too. How much would that suck? Ever since their late night at the diner, Gemma hadn't stopped thinking about Crystal. Actually, it was bordering on creepy the way she searched for the tiny brunette in crowds and constantly checked her cell phone for missed calls.

"'Scuse me."

Gemma tucked her legs under her chair as the supervising producer, Talia, stumbled past. Poor Talia. Her puffy eyes and devastated scowl pretty much confirmed Gemma's theory that she and James were an item. But it didn't get Gemma any closer to the truth. She slowly rose and tiptoed out of the room, walking down the hall in a daze. Her head was spinning. The fact that Ms. O'Shea wouldn't give an explanation probably meant there was a really juicy one, and that only made Gemma more curious. But what was it? Had James been embezzling money? Lying about sources? Banging the wrong *Back Talk*er?

BACK TALK

Gemma zombie-walked down the hall, halfway through hand-delivering a memo to each and every staff member. Ugh. She looked down at the stack of memos. It was thinning out, but so was her patience, and she was *so* ready for a coffee break. Dragging her feet like the sullen teenager she was, Gemma hummed Madonna's "Lucky Star" and handed memos to the accounting staff. The upshot—if you could call it that—was that she overheard a lot of juicy gossip as she breezed invisibly through the office.

"That's what I heard," Charlie the PR guy boasted to Val, Stacy, and Enid during a quick tête-à-tête in his cubicle.

"No!" Enid's eyes bulged dramatically. "What a tosser," she gasped in Brit-speak for *asshole.*

"I believe it," Val said, blowing on her piping-hot latte. "James is such a letch. It was only a matter of time before he sexually harassed someone."

Sexually did *what?* Gemma's jaw dropped but she snapped it shut, inching out of the room. If she walked slow enough, maybe she'd hear the victim's name.

"Yeah," Stacy agreed. "But Maria Cruz? She's kryptonite. He *had* to know her daddy would get him canned."

Talk about juicy gossip—you could make Popsicles out of that.

Gemma stumbled into the hallway. Sure, James acted like Sleazy McPervs-A-Lot, but she couldn't believe he'd actually harass someone. Her face crinkled up in disgust. God, if it *was* true? Eew! She'd been alone with him in the elevator, like, ten times. He could have … no. It was still possible that this was a big misunderstanding.

Gemma sprinted to Clark's office and tapped lightly on the door. "You got a sec?" If anyone had the 411, it was Clark Dobbs.

Clark nodded *yes* without taking his eyes off Oprah. Four to five p.m. was, like, the holy hour in Clark's '80s-themed office. Gemma tiptoed in, squatting on a hot pink, inflatable plastic chair, and watched Clark watch a fat blonde recount her grueling tale of being buried alive.

"What's up?" Clark asked, muting the TV at the commercial break. "Can you believe the James drama? It's better than *Days of Our Lives*!"

"That's what I wanted to talk to you about. Do you really think it's true?"

Clark leaned back in his chair and closed his office door. One can never be too careful. "Which story did you hear?"

"What do you mean?" Gemma asked. "There's more than one?"

"Well, Neela said he was caught stealing from petty cash. I also heard he hires actors instead of finding real guests. Oh, and my personal favorite: James knocked up Irene from accounting."

Irene from accounting was about seventy and smelled like bleu cheese. Now that's just sick.

"I heard he got fired for harassing Maria Cruz."

Clark shrugged ruefully. That was obviously the theory he subscribed to. "Seems pretty concrete," he sighed. "Apparently it happened in the office, late Friday."

Gemma shook her head angrily. "Seriously? What bullshit!"

"Methinks thou dost protest too much," Clark sang, raising his eyebrows.

"Is that Shakespeare?"

"Who cares," he waved dismissively. "You're missing the point. Look at you, all *outraged* and shit. What's your sitch?"

"I don't know." Gemma sighed and picked up a Rubik's cube off Clark's desk. "I overheard James one day. He was telling Talia how much he loathed the twins. Why would he turn around and, like, perv on them?"

"He'd tell Talia that Coco Chanel was his grandmother if it would get her panties off," Clark snickered. "But I know what you mean," he added quickly. "The way they were whoring themselves around at Nick's party? I mean, please. Who'd want to tap *that*?"

Gemma's eyes widened. "That's right!" She pushed herself out of the squeaky plastic chair and paced deliberately. Her little brain was working double time to piece together a new theory. "Who gets molested on Friday, then acts like it's *MTV Spring Break* on Saturday night?"

The girl had a good point. Insensitively phrased, but a good point.

Clark rubbed the small goatee growing on his chin. "I don't know. I love your Nancy-Drew-meets-*CSI-Miami* enthusiasm, but nobody's gonna buy it." He raised the volume on Oprah and resumed his infatuation with the buried-alive chick. "Just forget it, Gem."

Gemma sighed and sulked out of Clark's office. He was probably right. She should probably just forget it. But what were the chances of *that* happening?

NINETEEN

Gemma opened the front door to Dana's apartment, immediately stubbing her toe on a Louis Vuitton trunk. Why was a massive trunk blocking the door? She cursed it as she limped past, bending down to read the brown leather luggage tag: *America Vanderbilt*. Hmm... Gemma frowned nervously. A suitcase could mean any number of things, but her eager little brain immediately jumped to (a) a death in the family, or (b) a major blowout between Dana and America (with herself partially to blame). She dropped her purse on the trunk and ran down the hall, following voices to the kitchen.

The scene in the kitchen *definitely* implied scenario B, with little more than a wooden table standing between Dana and America and a brutal eye-scratching catfight.

"How can you say that?" America boomed. She hiked up the sleeves of her white, belted Chloe sundress and pounded her fists on the counter.

"Whatever, at least I'm not a superficial bitch," Dana laughed callously. She was enjoying this way too much. "I've stuck up for you so many times, and how do you repay me? By sleeping with my brother because he looks good on *paper*?" She shook her head incredulously. "Maybe you really *are* as shallow as everyone says."

"You hypocrite!" America fumed. "You sleep with guys like they're on sale at Barney's, and you're calling *me* a slut?"

Dana huffed and puffed and blew a wisp of hair out of her eyes. "That's different. I fall in love easily and sometimes I like to ... show it," she said cautiously, her voice softening. She leaned back in her black cropped jumpsuit, hoisting her body up onto the counter next to the sink. "But Danny is my whole *family*. What you did was heartless. I invite you to live in my home and in return you treat my brother like a male hooker or something!"

America's face reddened. A stray tear rolled down her cheek and she quickly brushed it away. "It doesn't matter anyway. Danny left for Tokyo this morning. And if it makes you feel any better, he saw through my *clever little plan*," she added wryly, dragging her feet to the breakfast table. She sighed heavily, mumbling almost inaudibly. "He didn't even say goodbye."

The room went eerily silent as America collapsed into a chair and buried her head in her hands. Either she was the next Meryl Streep or the girl was seriously upset. And whatever she was doing, it worked, because Dana abruptly pushed herself off the counter and inched her way toward America. This was a very unexpected turn of events. Dana fought with people all the time, but she rarely made them cry. The whole bitch-to-blubbering-baby thing had her flummoxed. She hovered behind America, debating whether to pat her on the shoulder or pick another fight.

"Is she *really* crying?" Dana mouthed to Gemma, still hovering in the doorway.

"I don't know," Gemma mouthed back. Suddenly she felt like the world's biggest asshole. To think, *she'd* instigated this whole thing by blabbing America's offhand confession about Danny to Dana. She bit her thumbnail repentantly, wishing she could take it all back.

"America?" she finally squeaked. "Are you okay?"

America's shoulders bobbed gently, but she wouldn't lift her head off the table.

"Sweetie?" Dana added, squatting on the chair next to America. "Look, I really didn't know it was this serious. When Gemma told me that stuff you said, I just thought..."

Rub it in, Gemma winced. She grabbed a box of tissues off the counter and set them next to America's head as a peace offering.

"I...fe...i-i-in...lo-lo-lo www..." America sobbed, slowly lifting her head. She looked like Rudolph on crack.

"One more time?" Dana asked, her face scrunched in confusion.

America grabbed the tissues and blew through six before opening her mouth again. She was a train wreck—and definitely *not* Meryl. "You guys, I don't know what to do. I think I'm seriously in love with him."

Gemma smiled giddily. "That's awesome!"

"Not quite, *genius*," America spat sarcastically. She ripped another tissue from the box and scowled at Gemma. "Because I told you my confused, insecure, teenage-girl feelings instead of just keeping my mouth shut, Danny thinks I'm this insensitive bitch who's after his money and social status—but hey, at least I got laid, right?" She laughed bitterly and narrowed her puffy eyes on Dana. "I guess I can thank you for waiting till the end of Danny's trip to let him in on my *master plan*."

Oops. Dana smiled apologetically. Maybe telling Danny instead of confronting America *hadn't* been the best idea, because right now, looking into America's weepy, bloodshot eyes, Dana felt about as helpful as *Chicken Soup for the Back-Stabbing Best Friend's Soul*. She sunk down in her chair and pouted dramatically. How was she supposed to know the whole thing would blow up in her face?

Clearly *Dawson's Creek* reruns have taught her nothing.

"This is all my fault. I'm *so* sorry," Gemma said gravely. She swallowed, feeling a lump form in the back of her throat. "I know I shouldn't have said anything, but ..." Tears of guilt and embarrassment tumbled down her cheeks and she quickly turned her head to face the wall. She couldn't bear to have her friends see her cry.

"Come on, Gemma," America sighed, grabbing another tissue and pushing the box across the table. "It's okay."

"No," Gemma sobbed, shaking her head violently. "You trusted me with your feelings and I broke that trust."

"Oh god," Dana groaned. "Overdramatic much? Can we all just kiss and make up before this turns into a Renée Zellweger movie?"

Gemma laughed through her tears and tried to curtail the sobs.

"That's better," Dana smiled. She turned, pouting ruefully at America. "I'm sorry I sabotaged your love life. What can I do to fix it?"

"Nothing," America shrugged, resting her cheek on her hands. "It's not like I can go to Japan to win him back."

Dana's eyes widened. "*Hellooo*, that's *exactly* what you can do!" She pushed herself up from the table and began pacing around the kitchen. "God, it's brilliant. He's crushed, and what's a bigger ego boost than a hot chick flying seven thousand miles to see you?"

"God, that sounds *so* romantic," Gemma gushed, dabbing her face with a tissue.

America rolled her eyes. "And so *not* me," she grumbled. "I have my pride. And if Danny can't even confront me before running off to Japan, then I'm not about to grovel."

True, America wasn't much for groveling.

"Everything okay, niñas? I heard crying," Gabriella said, peeking her head into the kitchen in a pink Juicy tracksuit— no doubt a hand-me-down of Reese Cox's.

"America's got boy trouble," Dana said, still pacing the length of the Tuscan-style kitchen.

Gabriella smiled in a you-crazy-kids kind of way and walked over to the fridge. "I got just the thing," she said, pulling out a tinfoil-covered dish. "I make my famous leche quemada. You try some?"

"Gabby, you're a goddess," Dana said, snatching the dish from the housekeeper's hands. "Gabby makes this insane fudge. I ate the whole thing once when I was totally sto—hungry." *Right.* She cut a few chunks of fudge and brought them over to the table on a small Nambé platter.

"Thanks." Gemma grabbed a piece and popped it in her mouth. It was probably five thousand calories, but an extra half hour on the treadmill should even it out. *Sure.*

"Thanks, Gabriella, but I'm not hungry." America frowned, staring disgustedly at the plate of sugar.

Gabriella nodded, replacing the tinfoil and sticking the block of fudge back in the fridge. She shuffled over and kissed America on the forehead. "You will feel better soon. Let your heart tell you what is best." She squinted, eyeing the girls thoughtfully, then headed for the door. "You kids think you must rush everything. Save yourself for the right time."

"Gracias, Gabriella." America smiled and watched her leave. No need to tell Gabriella that she'd stopped "saving herself" last year on her parents' yacht.

"Listen to your heart, my child," Gemma mimicked solemnly, licking her fudgy fingers.

America giggled and pinched a tiny morsel of fudge. Then she took a deep breath, wiping fresh tears from her face. She couldn't believe she'd broken down like that. There was a hard and fast rule about crying in the Vanderbilt household: don't—especially not in public. But the chances of this getting back to Deirdre and Lloyd Vanderbilt were slim to none, so America tried to let it go.

"So, Japan?" Dana prodded, pouring herself a tumbler of Perrier.

"Japan," America repeated in a daze. She looked up and blinked. "I don't think so. I've got my internship."

"*Yeah*," Dana snickered. She sat back at the table, dabbing fudge crumbs off the platter with her index finger. "Like they care if you miss a week of dusting off archival slides or whatever."

"Thanks." America sneered. "How about this. I'll go if you guys come with me."

Gemma shook her head dubiously—not that she didn't *want* to. Jetting off to Tokyo on a moment's notice sounded awesome. Sadly, back on planet Earth she had an actual job with commitments. A week in Japan might be frowned upon.

"Me neither. We start filming soon." Dana shrugged.

"At least call him," Gemma begged America. She couldn't bear to see true love die.

"I'll think about it," America mused. "But he won't be home till tomorrow anyway." She cleared her throat and straightened her posture, pushing the fudge out of her reach.

"Now, I'm sick of all the attention. Can we Dr. Phil someone else?"

"I'm thinking about having an affair with my director," Dana giggled.

"What?" Gemma gasped.

Only *Dana*.

"And what about the DJ you've been whining about for the past two weeks?" America challenged.

"He was hot," Dana admitted, "but unless he pulls his head out of his ass, I've got to explore my options."

"Your warped brain is too much for me," America sighed. "Just tell me the director's not Old Man River."

"Of course not," Dana promised. "He's twenty-seven."

"You do realize that he was *ten* when you were born, right?" Gemma piped in.

"You *do* realize you're annoying?" Dana mimicked, making a face. "And I'll *win* this fight. I've got practically all of Hollywood to back me up—Tom Cruise and Katie Holmes, Demi and Ashton … Armande Reno and Dana Cox—"

"*Armande?*" America drawled. "Tell me that's not his name. That's a gigolo's name, or a fat wino. I think my first chauffer was called Armande …"

"He's no chauffeur. But I wouldn't mind if he shifted *my* gears!"

"Oh *god*," Gemma shuddered with laughter. "You're like a boy."

Dana giggled, clapping for her own dirty little mind. "Yeah, but it'll probably never happen. I think he's M and K," she added, dropping her clever code for *M*arried with

Kids. Apparently it was a predicament she came across often enough to label. With a sigh, she popped a miniscule speck of fudge into her mouth and motioned to Gemma. "How about you, princess? Want to be Dr. Phil'd?"

"Yeah, if I *had* a love life," Gemma laughed pathetically. "The only person I sit around waiting for a phone call from is Crystal."

"You mean that psycho hooker who called you at, like, three a.m.?" Dana asked, confused. "Isn't it good that she's not calling?"

"Yeah," Gemma lied quickly. She smiled and looked out the window. What was the point in telling her high-society friends that she was tormented by the crumbling existence of a misunderstood prostitute? They totally wouldn't get it. "But I've got gossip..." she finally added, raising an eyebrow.

America and Dana perked up immediately.

"One of the producers at *Back Talk* was fired. And the story is..." she paused for dramatic effect, stealing a sip of Dana's water. "He sexually harassed one of the twins!"

Dana's eyes bulged. "*No!* I love it," she hooted, rubbing her hands together. "How tawdry."

"I know!" Gemma exclaimed, hugging her knees. "Not like this producer is a Boy Scout or anything, but I don't think he did it. The twins are just too annoying."

"I feel kind of bad for them," America said quietly.

"Huh?" Dana and Gemma asked.

America stood up and walked over to the kitchen window, gazing out onto Eighty-Third Street. "Their father is

Robert Cruz, right?" she asked. "He's powerful and preoccupied. They'd probably do anything to get his attention."

Gemma fell silent. America had that I-know-what-I'm-talking-about look again. For one thing, the girl never talked about her parents. From what Gemma gathered, the Vanderbilts weren't exactly the *Brady Bunch*. Actually, Dana knew all about messed-up family life, too. Her father was dead, her mother had abandoned her, and her stepbitch was—well, the nickname pretty much said it all.

"You're probably right," Gemma nodded sympathetically. "But why take James down, too?"

"I'm not *actually* Dr. Phil," America quipped. "But they're probably used to having their own way. If James blew them off, I bet they wanted revenge."

"You're good," Dana said, applauding America. "Dr. Phil's got nothin' on you."

"Oh, *stop*," America bragged, fanning herself.

Gemma sighed, stuffing the last chunk of fudge into her mouth. America was probably right, but it didn't make her feel any better. Actually, it made her feel worse. The pathetic, love-starved twins had ruined James's life just to get their daddy's attention. She folded her arms, sulking bitterly. It didn't seem fair.

TWENTY

It was a banner day at the old *Back Talk* office. With James out of the picture, the staffers were majorly freaking out and Gemma was *thiiis* close to having a meltdown. It was like everyone had come in early to smoke crack without letting her in on the plan.

Now *that* would make a good talk show.

Gemma sat nervously at the edge of her swivel chair, diligently logging footage in front of a video deck while busy bees buzzed around her in the PA room. It was a mini Times Square. All the computers were occupied, as were the copy machines, the fax, and the scanner. For Gemma, Hell had finally earned its name.

"Have you seen Anita or Maria?" Kamara asked, nudging Gemma. She walked over to the fax machine and tapped it expectantly with her pencil. "I really need their help with something."

Gemma cringed. So *that* was how her day could go from bad to worse—finding out that she was less useful than the twins. What a motivator. She shook her head and turned back to the TV, scribbling down time codes for a tape package on the Cronin family. It was actually a pretty sweet job. Gemma liked to think of it as doing the editor's dirty work. She found clips and noted the time codes for some other guy to string them together and add music. Ta-da!

"Gemma, I need those time codes!" Carla whined, marching into the room.

If Gemma thought *she* was stressed, then Carla was like the black hole of panic attacks. The girl's deep cocoa skin had turned pale and clammy, and massive sweat stains clung to the armpits of her gray cotton Vince T-shirt. Not pretty. She exchanged a knowing eye roll with Kamara and stomped toward the TV, scowling down at Gemma and drumming her acrylic nails urgently against the TV stand. "Are you done yet? When will you be done?"

That crack-smoking theory was starting to hold some ground…

"One minute," Gemma cowered. She hit fast forward and tried without success to ignore Carla's menacing presence. The woman was like an evil schoolteacher critiquing Gemma's grammar.

"Did you write that down?" Carla barked, tapping the screen at a clip of Mrs. Cronin and her now-deceased daughter opening Christmas presents. "Because that was a good shot. If you didn't get it, I don't know *how*—"

"I got it," Gemma snapped testily.

Gemma pursed her lips and took a slow, steady breath, focusing her attention on the Cronin's dismal life. She'd been logging these stupid home movies for over two hours and there was enough Christmas morning footage for a third remake of *Miracle on 34th Street*. "There was a better shot earlier on, so I grabbed that time code instead," she explained as evenly as possible.

"Fine," Carla growled, scanning the room. "Where are the twins?"

Again with the twins? Gemma was starting to get a complex. "I don't know. But here," she said, pressing eject on the VCR. She handed the video and time codes to Carla and stood up slowly. "Mind if I take a quick break?" Her ass was falling asleep.

Before Carla could answer, the speak-of-the-twin-devils bounced into the room wearing matching Betsy Johnson sundresses and giggling like it *wasn't* the apocalypse. Gemma smiled inwardly as all the bustling activity came screeching to a halt, from the whirring copy machines to the clickity-clicking keyboards. Everyone stopped to glare at the twins. Apparently Gemma wasn't the only one who thought Maria made up the sexual harassment claim. But slowly everyone got back to work. They were a bunch of chicken shits and, sadly, steady income took precedence over justice.

Gemma slipped past the twins and lingered by the coat-rack to eavesdrop. She could pretend she was beyond petty jealousy but it would be a lie, and she was dying to know what Kamara and Carla needed the twins for so badly. It helped her sanity.

"What?" Maria whined defensively. She pulled her long, chestnut hair into a clip at the base of her neck and sat on the edge of Bobby's desk, throwing him a cutesy wink.

"*What?*" Carla repeated indignantly. "Oh *nothing*. We're just trying to produce a talk show. Maybe you've heard of it, it's called—"

"Uh, hey Anita!" Kamara jumped in, quickly saving Carla from forced early retirement. "We need clean copies of the Crystal Bloom article. I did a quick search, but since you found it initially, I figured you could grab it."

Anita's face turned three shades whiter than the faded ecru walls.

Kamara pushed herself away from the fax machine, grabbing the incoming fax she'd been waiting for, and turned back to Anita. "Just make twenty copies and drop them on my desk ASAP."

Before Kamara could catch her hovering by the coats like an idiot, Gemma ran to the bathroom and locked herself in the corner stall. She put the lid down and sat on it, hugging her knees to her chest. Her eyes were fried from Cronin overload and she couldn't get over how mad those stupid twins made her. *Pathetic*, Gemma sighed, dizzying herself with the squiggly print of her Missoni knockoff dress.

The bathroom door swung open and Gemma stiffened. It was the twins—shock of all shocks. God, they were the absolute *bane* of her existence.

"Would you snap out of it?" Maria hissed.

Through the crack in the door Gemma watched Maria bend down to check the stalls for feet and thanked her lucky stars she was hugging her knees to her chest. This all felt very secret agency.

"What are we supposed to do?" Anita whimpered. "If Kamara finds out we—"

"Nobody's going to find out, dorkwad," Maria promised, pinching her cheeks in the mirror. "All we have to do is find the stupid article. If Gemma did it, how fucking hard could it be?"

Gemma covered her mouth, stifling an enraged gasp. Her face burned with embarrassment as she realized that those tacky, conniving bitches had confirmed her paranoid suspicions: they'd stolen her prostitute article. Sweat trickled down Gemma's back as she crouched on the toilet seat, trying not to literally explode with anger.

Maria pulled a burgundy lipstick out of her pocket and puckered her bubble lips into a giant O. "But you can't freak out like that. Bobby was starting to look suspicious, and if we can't fool *Bobby*, then we totally suck."

Anita nodded, sniffing back a tear.

"Okay?" Maria smiled, kissing her reflection. She handed the lipstick to Anita and shifted her breasts in her geranium print dress. "Nobody knows I ganked Gemma's article.

I think I even remember a few key words from it so all we have to do is find it online and we're back on track." She spun on her heels and sashayed toward the door.

Anita sniffled again, glowering at her sister's back. Popping out of the womb two minutes after Maria had caused years of mental anguish and insecurity. Anita wasn't likely to move on. Cursing quietly under her breath, she threw her lipstick tube in the sink and stalked out of the ladies room.

Ho-ly. *Shit*. Gemma was floored. If she'd been wired by the FBI, that information might *actually* have been useful, but who'd take the word of a sixteen-year-old intern? The odds weren't good.

For another ten minutes, Gemma sat in her stall reading office graffiti and scratching her chin. So the twins lied about the article... Interesting. What else had they been lying about? She was sitting on a frigging goldmine of information—at least *she* thought so. Now she just had to figure out what she was going to do with it.

TWENTY-ONE

Gemma pulled the lid off of her caramel Frappuccino and took a gulp, licking sticky whipped cream off her upper lip. It was just what she needed after a harrowing day. She took another sip and scanned Starbucks for a seat, somewhat disheartened by the corporate lack of atmosphere. Where were all the cute loveseat-and-overstuffed-pillow-filled coffee houses? A lot of people are misled by Central Perk from *Friends*, and Gemma was one of them.

Could you be loved, and be loved. Gemma hummed along with the Bob Marley tune playing over a PA as she collapsed onto a stool by the window, lazily sipping her Frappuccino and half-reading a tattered copy of *Jude the Obscure*—not for fun. It was, like, *the* most depressing book ever, but she wanted to get ahead for senior AP English. She kicked off her silver ballet flats and stretched out her toes like a cat. Time to zone out.

"Hey!"

A sudden knock on the window made her flinch. The chances of it being anyone *other* than a homeless guy were slim, so when she looked into the soft brown eyes of the adorable, Jonathan Rhys Meyers-esque Subway Guy, Gemma thought she was going to die of a heart attack.

"May I join you?" he mouthed, brushing a longish strand of brown hair out of his eyes.

Before Gemma knew what was happening, Subway Guy was inside Starbucks and weaving his way toward her. She quickly slipped back into her flats and dug around in her bag for some lipstick, begging herself not to royally fuck this up.

Kind of a tall order.

She smiled as he drew closer, internally humming the *Jaws* theme. There were probably a million things she could say to him, but of course Gemma—like a freakish science experiment gone wrong—couldn't think of a single one. Their only conversation to date had been about prostitutes. How do you top *that*?

Subway Guy dropped his mailbag on the floor and pulled up a stool, smiling comfortably at Gemma. "Awright," he said in his boisterous English accent.

Assuming "awright" meant "all right," did "all right" mean "hello"? Gemma couldn't be sure. She self-consciously squirmed on her stool, briefly trying to picture a tranquil stream or a rainbow or whatever people thought about to calm down.

Yeah, like *that* worked.

Subway Guy grinned and tousled his hair. Mmm, he was still using that yummy, sweet-smelling shampoo. He rolled up the cuffs of his white button-down shirt and smiled at Gemma's intrigue in the funky *W* tattoo on his forearm.

"Have you ever been tot'lly bollocksed and done something you wished you hadn't?" he asked mischievously.

Who? Gemma?

She scratched her elbow thoughtfully. It was too bad she'd left her Brit-speak dictionary at home, but she could pretty much guess that bollocksed meant drunk. She shrugged coquettishly hoping vague flirtation would suffice.

"Well, one afternoon after a few too many pints, my mates and I got tattoos. Mine's the Weezer logo. Their last album was rubbish, but I'm still a fan. D'you like Weeza'?"

Gemma nodded enthusiastically. Same taste in music. She had tingles. "I forgot that was their logo. Did it hurt?"

He shook his head, pulling a bottle of water out of his bag. "Not as much as the bloody hangover!"

"Gotta love a drunken escapade," Gemma giggled. She futzed with the strap of her sundress and let herself stare into his deep brown eyes. She wasn't ready to pen a self-help book or anything, but there was definitely some confidence coursing through those veins.

"Oh shit," Subway Guy said, smacking his forehead. "I haven't introduced myself. You must think I'm a complete wanker." He held out his hand to Gemma. "I'm Joseph Cross. Just Joe."

Gemma's entire arm tingled as she shook Joe's hand. "I don't know what a wanker is, so you're off the hook. I'm Gemma…" She'd hold out on the "Winters" part till she knew him better. "It's nice to meet you, Just Joe."

Joe grinned and shook his head.

"What?" Gemma tucked her brown locks behind her ears anxiously.

"Nothing." He rested his elbow on the counter and put his head in his hand, staring at Gemma. "I'm just chuffed to see you again," he said sheepishly.

In a perfect world, Gemma would have said she was happy to see him, too—or *anything at all* for that matter—but you know how it is… old dog, new tricks, yada yada. She managed a demure smile before lowering her head shamefully. *Could I be any worse at this?*

"I'm sorry," Joe apologized. "I—"

"No," Gemma sputtered, touching his thigh before she knew what she was doing. She retracted it just as quickly and sucked down a mouthful of Frappuccino to buy some time. "I… I'm a little socially awkward, if you hadn't already guessed."

"I think you're lovely," he said sweetly.

Swoon. Gemma looked down at her cup to hide her burning cheeks.

Joe smiled at the adorably quirky, self-conscious girl he'd found and took a swig of water. "Let's see," he mused. "Last time I saw you, you were trawling for prostitutes. Haven't changed careers, I hope?"

"No!" Gemma laughed, embarrassed. "But I did have coffee with a thirteen-year-old hooker."

"Shit, how do I top that?" Joe asked, scratching his chin. "She's going to be on your show, then, yeah? That's bloody brilliant."

Gemma nodded. Joe had a good memory and she was thrilled to see him so interested in Crystal's story—or at least the girl telling the story.

"It's wicked that you're helping her change her life," Joe gushed. "She'll have you to thank when she becomes president."

"I wouldn't go *that* far," Gemma said, rolling her eyes modestly. "It was a total fluke that I got to know Crystal. But she's incredible. I can't believe *I'm* older than *her*. She's had experiences I've only read about in books." Gemma blushed, realizing that her eyes must be glistening with admiration for a thirteen-year-old streetwalker. She grabbed her Frappuccino and shrugged. "I'm just a lowly intern and resident photocopy bitch. It's all very glamorous." She fluttered her fingers like a Broadway chorus girl. Jazz hands helped emphasize the irony in her voice.

"Aw, don't sell yourself short," Joe said earnestly.

Gemma grinned up at Mr. Perfect. A tiny paranoid voice in the back of her head reminded her that Nick had been this perfect in the beginning, too, but she disregarded it. Joe was a thousand times sweeter, kinder, and less arrogant than

Nick. She smiled, wondering if she could bottle the guy for mass production.

"What's that, then?" Joe asked as Gemma absently fanned herself with *Jude the Obscure*. She handed him the book and watched him practically guffaw in amazement.

Uh, okay, *freakshow*. Gemma frowned as Joe plummeted from a ten to a seven on her perfect-o-meter. How could anyone get *that* excited over *that* book?

"Sorry," Joe apologized, suddenly aware of Gemma's bewildered scowl. He put the book on the table and slid it across to her. "It's just that *Jude the Obscure* is by Thomas Hardy. He's from my hometown."

"Really?" Gemma marveled. "How funny is that! Where?"

"Oh, you'll never've heard of it, but I'm from Dorchester. In a county called Dorset," he added.

Damn, Gemma didn't have her Brit-speak dictionary *or* her Brit-map. She nodded anyway, a confused smile plastering her face.

He chuckled, obviously used to the reaction. "It's all right. Half the people in England don't know where it is. It's near the seaside, southwest of London."

Gemma nodded, trying not to explode from the possibility that this might be fate.

"D'you like it, then?" Joe asked, gesturing toward *Jude*.

"I've never been a big fan of incest and infanticide, but other than that…"

"Right," Joe chuckled, pushing up his sleeves again. "That's English lit'rature for you. We're not happy unless everyone's dead or insane. But it's not all like that—Agatha Christie, Shakespeare, Roald Dahl..."

"That's true," Gemma giggled. "I love Roald Dahl. I'm probably not supposed to admit it, but I love children's books."

"You can admit it to me," Joe whispered with a wink. "I've got my own secret addiction to Harry Potter." He slowly ran a palm over his brown hair, realizing his faux pas. "It's not a secret anymore when I blurt it out!"

"I'll take it to the grave," Gemma promised, locking her mouth and throwing the key over her shoulder. She looked out the window and smiled at an apple-cheeked baby going past in a stroller. "So," she began slowly, looking back at Joe. "What do you do—other than read Harry Potter and get drunken Weezer tattoos?"

"I'm starting at Columbia in September," Joe reported, putting his empty water bottle back in his bag. He took out a pack of Trident and handed a piece to Gemma. "But for the summer I'm working at my uncle's music shop, Metro Records."

Gemma coughed violently.

"You all right?" Joe asked. Gemma popped the gum into her mouth and motioned for him to continue. "I want to be a musician," Joe continued. "I had a band in school. It was a Sex Pistols cover band. Bloody awful, but we had fun!"

Gemma laughed at the mental image of "Joe Vicious." Frightening. But kinda hot.

"Anyway, I love New York. I've never been to America before."

Gemma's eyes popped. She'd never *left* America before.

"Some of the people drive me bonkers, though," Joe admitted. "Everyone's in such a bloody rush."

"I know," Gemma sympathized. She'd said the exact same thing to Dana and America, but they didn't get it. "I'm from a small town, too."

"Coun'ry livin' innit?" Joe drawled. Then he laughed, both at his joke and at the fact that Gemma didn't get it.

"Sorry. *Country living, isn't it?*" he enunciated. "My Britishisms must get fuck-off annoying. My new flatmates tell me I'm a country bumpkin. I'm trying to tone it down, but you should hear my mates from Dorset. They're like English rednecks, yeah?"

Gemma laughed. "I'd need a translator in Dorset, wouldn't I?"

"I could be your translator," Joe blushed.

He was almost too adorable.

Gemma blushed back at him then peered out the window, admiring the orangy glow of the sunset. She indulged in a twenty-second fantasy of their first romantic English countryside picnic, complete with wine, cheese, flowers, a little David Gray on the radio … Mmm.

"I better go," Gemma blurted abruptly. She put *Jude the Obscure* back into her bag and hopped off the stool, tossing her empty Frappuccino cup into the trash. What was she supposed to do next? Never having met her dream guy before, she was a little unsure. Would it be proper etiquette to throw him down on the counter and ravage him? Doubtful. But she'd definitely say yes if he asked her out.

Joe got up, too, slinging his mailbag over his shoulder. "Listen, Gemma," he hesitated. "I've got a gig Thursday night at Dark Room, this lounge on the Lower East Side. A couple of my mates are popping 'round and I wondered if you'd come, too? It should be a laugh."

Gemma bit her lip to keep from screaming. That kinda sounded like a date. She smiled giddily, wishing she could reach up and nuzzle her face in his neck and kiss him like crazy.

Jesus Christ, do it already.

"That sounds cool," Gemma said. She followed Joe outside, hoping her breezy response hadn't come across as aloof. Gemma pulled her hair into a loose bun and tilted her head back, basking in the sultry evening air. It was humid and hot but a welcome change from over-air-conditioned Starbucks. "You don't still sound like the Sex Pistols, right?" she asked, as they both turned north. "I'm a little more Johnny *Cash* than Johnny *Rotten*."

Joe laughed. "Don't worry. The Sex Pistols was a just phase, thank god."

They walked up Columbus Avenue in silence and Gemma felt her blood rush with adrenaline every time Joe's hand lightly scraped against hers. She wished they could keep walking forever...but she really had to pee.

"This is me," Gemma said, pointing vaguely east. Joe was probably perfect, but she was hesitant to give him her exact address.

What? It's not like he was going to write her a letter.

"Okay," Joe smiled. "I've had a brilliant time with you, Gemma."

Damn he had the cutest accent. And the cutest ears. Gemma didn't even have a thing for ears, but Joe's stuck out just the tiniest bit. And she loved the small silver hoop on the top of his right ear. She put her hands in her pockets to stop herself from tugging on those cute little lobes.

"Me too, Just Joe," Gemma giggled.

They stood awkwardly on the sidewalk. How was the goodbye gonna go down? A wave, a handshake, a hug? Answering her conundrum, Joe took Gemma's delicate hand into his calloused, guitar-player hand and lightly kissed it.

"So, Thursday then, yeah?" Joe asked, still holding Gemma's hand like it was Cinderella's glass slipper.

"At Dark Room," Gemma said, nodding firmly. She batted her eyelashes for good measure.

Joe released Gemma's hand and gave her a mini-salute, continuing up Columbus while she turned east toward the park. If it hadn't been for that pesky gravitational pull, she probably would have floated away.

TWENTY-TWO

Ding. The elevator doors opened onto the sixth floor and Gemma flew out like a headless chicken. The show-day vibe around *Back Talk* was insta-panic, especially for the already jinxed prostitution show. Apparently there were some vitally important papers needed by Leah, the staff lawyer, and Gemma was on a mission to find her, *stat.*

The hallway split off in three directions and Gemma panicked, choosing the sterile, white linoleum corridor to the left past a row of green metal doors. Aha! Finally she spotted Leah with Kamara outside hair and makeup and handed the willowy, pregnant brunette a stack of jargony-looking documents.

"Great," Leah said, flipping through the stack and waddling away. "I need Penelope's John Hancock on these ASAP. Good luck today," she added, winking at Kamara.

Kamara waved and turned to Gemma, a weary scowl on her face. "Are you busy? I need you to collect IDs from guests," she said in a tortured but firm voice. Then she sighed, squeezing her skull dramatically. "Our ex-prostitute brought triplet toddlers and no babysitter, so guess who gets to play Mary fucking Poppins all day?"

"Ouch." Gemma smiled sympathetically. "And don't worry about the IDs."

"Thanks." Kamara sighed again. "Just tell the guests we need Xeroxes for legal purposes. If you have any problems, ask Carla. I think she's prepping guests." Kamara took off her white Diesel blazer and tied it around her waist in preparation for battle. "You can make the copies at the machine down the hall in 609-A. And *don't* lose them."

Sir, yes sir.

Back Talk with Kate Morgan had five separate greenrooms where the guests could change and relax until they were called on set. Gemma always thought it sounded so glamorous, but in reality the greenrooms were tiny, fluorescent, and grubby. They weren't even green.

She walked down the hall cursing her paper-thin H&M sundress as she rubbed her arms for warmth. The studio was set at a constant fifty-eight degrees for all the equipment, which seemed ridiculous to Gemma and her goosebumps. What, like the spotlights were going to spontaneously combust?

Gemma passed Kate Morgan's dressing room on her right and peeked in. The room looked empty. Damn her curiosity! She tiptoed in, ogling bouquets of fragrant roses and calla lilies and a massive buffet table stocked with goodies from Dean & Deluca and Godiva. Framed pictures lined the walls: Kate with Madonna, Kate with Hilary Clinton, Kate with Jude Law. Kate Morgan had the life.

But Gemma had a job. She stopped fondly caressing Kate's Daytime Emmy and slipped out of her dressing room, hurrying toward the greenrooms to collect IDs—a boring but perk-laden activity thanks to Mrs. Cronin and her baking abilities. The woman had brought two baskets of chocolate chip cookies for the entire staff. She must have been at it for days and they were yummy as hell. Gemma ate two. Okay, four.

Licking gooey chocolate off her thumb and index finger, she walked down the hall toward the last ID she needed: Crystal Bloom's. To be honest, Gemma doubted if Crystal even *had* a driver's license. Birth certificate, maybe? She inched toward the greenroom, spotting Carla and Timothy arguing outside Crystal's door.

"…didn't mention anything?" Timothy snapped, shoving his hands in the pockets of his pressed chinos.

"When I talked to her yesterday she told me…" Carla's voice became a whisper and then picked back up again. "…going to kill her."

"Well, I don't have time…" Garble, garble. "…the show!"

Gemma heaved a frustrated sigh. How was she supposed to eavesdrop with all that whispering? She wasn't a goddamn lip reader. But something was definitely wrong, and it had to do with Crystal. Gemma took a few quick, deep breaths to psych herself up and marched up to Timothy and Carla.

Who died and gave her balls?

"I couldn't help overhearing. Is something wrong?" Gemma asked timidly.

Timothy's disgusted glare said it all. Even Gemma had to remind herself that she was a human being and not a three-headed sewer mutant. She crossed her arms awkwardly, wondering what the chances were of the floor opening up and swallowing her whole.

"Nothing an intern can help with," he finally spat, rolling his eyes judgmentally.

Ouch. Gemma bit her lip to keep from crying. She was an intern, not a leper. Although some days there wasn't much of a difference.

"Hold up," Carla said, tapping Timothy's shoulder. "Gemma might be able to help. She actually met Crystal. You two had coffee, right?"

Gemma nodded meekly.

"*You're* friends with that hooker?" Timothy scoffed dubiously. He put his hands on his hips, practically daring Gemma to elaborate.

"W-w … Well, she—I …"

"W-w-w-what are you trying to say?" Timothy spat heartlessly.

"We think Crystal bailed on the show," Carla interjected, saving Gemma from further humiliation. She pulled a pack of Rolaids out of her black slacks and popped two in her mouth. "She came by yesterday for her honorarium but I haven't talked to her since and she's not answering her cell phone. If you can think of *anything*..."

Gemma nodded in thought, following Carla and Timothy down the hall and onto the elevator. Unnerving silence filled the air as they ascended to the twenty-third floor. Off the top of her head, no, nothing came to mind, but Gemma kept thinking. She drummed her fingers against her arm methodically. *Crystal likes veggie burgers.* It was probably beside the point, but Gemma let the domino effect play out in her head: Crystal was a vegetarian because her father had taught her about slaughterhouses. Her father was the one person she missed. Maybe Crystal went to visit her dad's grave. Gemma toyed with the idea, but Crystal was from Colorado. Pretty far just to visit a cemetery.

Gemma tugged furiously at the silver bracelet wrapped around her wrist. There was the girl Crystal had run away from home with, but Gemma couldn't remember the kid's name. Useless.

As the elevator crept up, Gemma pleaded with her brain. She thought about the sugar sculpture Crystal had made at the diner. And Crystal's camera—*Crystal's camera*...photography...South Street Seaport.

"That's it!" Gemma exploded in unison with the elevator bell.

Timothy yanked Gemma into the hallway and grabbed her shoulders, thrusting his pointy little J. Crew model face in hers. "Spit it out, Jenna!"

"South Street Seaport," Gemma yelped.

Timothy let go of her shoulders and sprinted down the hall toward his office.

"Crystal wants to be a photographer," she yelled after him. "She goes to South Street to take pictures and stuff."

Timothy was a good twenty feet ahead but he beckoned for the girls to follow.

"Any calls?" Carla asked Melissa as they raced through the reception area.

Melissa shrugged apologetically.

They caught up to Timothy in his office and stood by as he flung open a file cabinet, busily rifling through a stack of papers. "South Street Seaport?" he repeated, grabbing a sheet of paper and slapping it confidently. "Find her, then get her to sign this, and we'll have her ass in a sling!" he roared, apparently forgetting that he was talking about a thirteen-year-old girl and not a bail jumper. "Take a Nextel. Call when you know anything." With bulging eyes, Timothy walked back around his desk and pushed the girls toward the door. "Let's *do* this!"

BACK TALK

Gemma's dark brown eyes drifted over hordes of tourists as a sickly feeling rose up in her stomach. They'd been combing South Street Seaport for twenty minutes and still there was no sign of Crystal. Maybe she hadn't said Seaport. Or maybe she had and she just wasn't there. All Gemma could be one hundred percent sure of was that her feet were killing her and she really wanted one of Carla's Rolaids.

"I don't see her," Carla whined, airing out her James Perse T-shirt. "Do you?"

Gemma didn't answer. Shielding the sun from her eyes, she squinted at a flock of tourists crowded around a five-year-old breakdancer. She took a few steps closer. At this point every short brunette looked like Crystal, but there was one in particular... Gemma squeezed Carla's arm, nodding toward a five-foot-two tan brunette in short-shorts and a pink tube top. The girl sat hunched over a railing, a familiar LeSportsac overnighter at her feet and a camera slung around her neck.

Bingo.

The girls crept toward Crystal like hunters zeroing in on their prey.

"Crystal?" Gemma said softly. She took another step closer and gasped. Crystal had a bruise the size of a tangerine around her left eye. Kenny's handiwork, no doubt.

Without a word Crystal hopped off the rail and took off at lightning speed. Before Gemma knew what was happening, Crystal was fifty feet away, but Carla grabbed Gemma's arm and they ran after her. It was hard to keep up, what with the thousands of tourists milling around with video cameras and maps, but Carla was unstoppable. She was like a football player, ramming people with her shoulders as she tore through the masses. Crystal continued to bob-and-weave through the tourists, finally slowing down near a pretzel stand to catch her breath.

"Crystal, we just want to talk to you," Carla yelled, gunning the last twenty feet.

"Leave me alone," Crystal pleaded in a steely voice.

"What happened?" Gemma asked, panting heavily. "Was it Kenny?"

Crystal grunted, shaking like a leaf. She wasn't about to tell two TV producers what was going on in her head. That would mean she trusted them, and trusting people wasn't really her *thing*. She pulled her bag off her shoulder and slunk over to an empty picnic table, hugging her knees tightly to her chest. "He's going to kill me," she finally choked, wiping away a tear. "I can't go on your show."

Carla and Gemma exchanged concerned looks. "Let us help you," Carla begged.

"Yeah?" Crystal snorted with laughter and crossed her arms. "*How?*"

Carla tugged at her slacks and sat on the bench next to Crystal. "I know it's scary, but you don't want to end up like this," she whispered. "Ten tricks a night? Handing every dime over to that sleaze ball? There are thousands of girls on the streets just like you, but we're giving *you* a chance. A chance to get out. Be strong, Crystal. Be a role model for the girls that can't stand up for themselves. They *need* you."

Cue violins.

Gemma smiled encouragingly. The speech was a bit cliched, but Crystal's eyes were glistening, and hey, if it got the job done ... Gemma sat on the other side of Crystal and gently stroked her back. She wanted to say something, but what? *Sorry your pimp beat you?* Growing up in the sticks next to a celebrity ski resort had hardly prepared her for this.

"We need you on that show today," Carla insisted. "Kate Morgan needs you. Listen, I wasn't supposed to tell you this ..." Carla waited for a flicker of interest in Crystal's eyes. "We've got something huge planned for today. A surprise. We got you into a school! It's this amazing specialized boarding school in upstate New York."

"*Boarding* school?" Crystal spat belligerently. "Is that code for, like, expensive?"

"No," Carla laughed. "We told the school all about you and," she looked around dramatically, checking for eavesdroppers and spies. It was all part of her grand plan to reel Crystal in and it was *so* working. Crystal's mouth was practically hanging open. "They're giving you a *full* scholarship! You'll have to take some aptitude tests and stuff, but I'm telling you this place is off the chain. They're all about education, life skills, the arts ..."

Crystal pushed herself off the bench and paced slowly, biting furiously at her thumbnail. "What about Kenny?"

Carla shook her head firmly. "Don't worry about him. After the show today, you're going to be, like, three hundred miles away. I guaran-fucken-tee he'll be in jail by the end of the week. We've put twenty criminals behind bars because of the Kate Morgan show."

Crystal took a deep breath and her shoulders dropped two inches. Wiping another tear from her cheek, she let out a choked giggle and nodded self-consciously.

All in a day's work. Seriously, how was Gemma not getting paid for this? She heaved a sigh of relief and rose to her feet, wiping a dribble of sweat off her neck.

"Now, can we haul your booty back to the studio?" Carla begged. "We've got a show to do."

Miraculously, the show only started a half hour late.

The girls rushed Crystal to hair and makeup where Shauna and Pat foundationed and hair sprayed her to death; then on to Gale from wardrobe who debated throwing Crystal in khaki slacks and a blue button-down, but found her tube top and short-shorts to be so deliciously déclassé. By the end, little Crystal was a walking, talking Trailer Trash Barbie.

After that, Timothy swooped in like Napoleon, only thinner and less French. "Always react," he instructed, whipping through a mountain of cue cards.

Talk show tip #17: The key to a good show is a well-briefed guest, and a well-briefed guest is a guest who knows the dramatic emphasis of her story.

"If you have something to say, jump in! Don't make Katie do all the talking. And when you're telling your story, remember: *it's sad!*" Timothy's exaggerated pouty face was almost Vaudevillian. "It's okay to cry. It'll make the audience more sympathetic to your plight."

Like Crystal knew what her *plight* was.

A tall black woman in mom-jeans and a Tweety Bird fleece poked her head into the greenroom and whistled. "You're up, baby," Rosie the stage manager purred. She jerked her head toward the door and cupped Crystal's hand in hers.

Timothy flicked through his note cards one last time and held his breath dramatically as his crucial Segment One guest disappeared down the hall.

Gemma tiptoed quietly behind as Rosie led Crystal under an illuminated ON AIR sign and down a pitch-black hallway. "When Kate introduces you," Rosie whispered, "you're going to walk up those stairs and onto the set." Their eyes had adjusted to the light and Rosie pointed to three steps covered in beige carpet leading out onto the classy, modern deco stage. "Kate will be in the leather chair, so you just sit on the sofa. You'll be fine, baby. Just relax." She gave Crystal a big warm mama-bear-looking-out-for-her-cub hug and ushered her to the sound guy for a quick microphone check.

The *Back Talk with Kate Morgan* theme music swelled through the studio—think Kenny G. meets Beyoncé. A nervous giggle escaped Gemma's lips and some asshole with a headset and a walkie-talkie shooed her out. No talking backstage was kind of a given. She hurried to the control room just in time to see Kate Morgan glide on stage in a gorgeous Nanette Lepore tweed suit and sassy knee-high boots. She was a breathtaking modern-day Marilyn. If she ever went back to Hollywood, Julia Roberts would be stuck with roles like Nurse #2. After a brief introduction of the show topic, Kate instigated a round of applause from the audience and introduced her prized guest.

Crystal needed a little nudge from Rosie but finally appeared onstage, squinting in the harsh glow of the 2000-watt stage lights. Talk about a deer caught in headlights. She held her elbows tightly to her chest and walked toward her designated spot next to Kate Morgan.

Gemma read the chyron at the bottom of the screen: *Thirteen-year-old Crystal has been a prostitute since age twelve.* The statement looked so clinical, like the warning label on a bottle of aspirin. Kind of anticlimactic after everything they'd been through to get her there.

"Crystal," Kate began in a warm but serious tone. "Three years ago you had the typical life, wouldn't you say?" She paused for Crystal's nod. "But then your father died. That must have been *devastating* for you."

Again, Crystal nodded.

"Please." Kate reached over and squeezed Crystal's hand. "Tell us, in your own words, how your life changed after that."

The show's about teen hookers, how do you *think* her life changed?

With a harrowing sigh, Crystal tucked her short brown hair behind her ears and let it *aaaall* out, from her stepfather's abuse, to running away, to meeting Kenny, to her first trick. Her performance was Oscar worthy. And Kate Morgan's slack-jawed audience ate it up. Daytime Emmy, here we come.

From the control room, Gemma avidly split her attention between Crystal on the monitors and the techie industry freaks around her. There was Penelope O'Shea, perched on a swivel chair in the back of the room with a mug of herbal tea and a line of pestering staffers at her feet. Behind a glass wall in the makeshift break room a few tech guys gathered around a platter of donuts arguing over an insignificant audio malfunction. Down in front, the director, Vince (the Viking), stood larger than life behind a wooden podium, interchangeably yelling "Cut to camera one," "Close-up on Crystal," and "Get a reaction shot of Katie" into his headset. There was the chyron operator, the still store operator, the assistant director, the lawyer, the script supervisor, and ten others puttering around.

"Unbelievable," Kate gasped upon hearing that Crystal performed up to ten "tricks" a night.

Crystal stifled a sob. Damn, Timothy's advice really paid off. Crystal's hardened, urban slang had a nice yin-yang thing going on with her subtle bursts of innocence. And the Segment Two surprise was killer. No one would have guessed that Carla had already let the cat out of the bag.

"Crystal," Kate said. Dramatic pause. "If you could have anything, *anything* at all, what would it be?"

Crystal stared down at her trashy platform wedges and sniffled. "I just want an education," she choked. "I want to be a photographer. I wanna go all over the world."

Kate Morgan smiled, nodding sympathetically. "Maybe work for *National Geographic* someday?" she prodded. She looked out compassionately at her audience and took a long, slow, deep breath.

Drag … It … Out … *More.*

"Well…" she finally said, turning back to Crystal. "We've got a surprise for you, Crystal." A sneaky grin spread across her face. "The generous dean at the Ramsey School in Albany, New York, has offered to give you a full, four-year scholarship!"

The audience roared into massive applause, complete with standing ovation and buckets-o-tears. Then the plasma screen stage left projected generic B-roll of the Ramsey campus and its students. While that was going on Kate reached behind her chair and whipped out a red-and-white Ramsey sweatshirt, handing it to a bewildered Crystal.

"Thanks," Crystal whispered, accepting the sweatshirt. She traced the letters with her pudgy fingers. "I don't believe it." She threw her arms around Kate's neck and practically mauled her in appreciation, shouting, "Holy shit!"

Don't worry, that'll get beeped out in post.

"Congratulations, sweetie," Kate giggled, returning the hug. "I know it's going to be a difficult adjustment, but you're a tough cookie. And you'll be safe there. We've made sure of that. You don't have to worry about your pimp coming after you." She gave Crystal one last squeeze and turned to camera one. "Log onto our website to find out more about the Ramsey School. Up next: an ex-prostitute who's making a difference," Kate said cryptically, smiling till they cut to commercial.

Not a dry eye in the house—well, except for the jaded techs and execs. They all looked a little constipated. What was with all the callous and bitter industry vets, anyway?

Was there no crying in TV land? Maybe not, but for everyone else it was a four-hankie event.

Gemma snatched a napkin off the donut table and wiped her eyes, grabbing another napkin to blow her nose. She couldn't stop replaying Crystal's big moment in her head. She'd put a lot of work into that show, and if she wanted to turn on the waterworks, who was going to stop her?

TWENTY-THREE

"Toast!" cheered the tipsy happy-hour crowd. They whooped wildly, pounding their fists against the beer-soaked tables at RubyBar.

Penelope O'Shea modestly declined. She stuck out like Mother Teresa at a wet T-shirt contest but she showed her camaraderie by sucking the olive out of her Belvedere martini and downing it in one gulp. It only made her look more desperate, but that in itself was kind of entertaining.

"Hey girls!" Clark said, bumping into Gemma and Dana as he sidled up to the bar. "Two whiskey sours," he added to the bartender. "Congrats on the show, by the way."

Gemma smiled. "Really? Thanks. Do you think Kate Morgan liked it?"

"Are you kidding? She loved it," Clark hollered. "Loved the guests, loved the surprises, loved the message. Loved it, loved it, *loved* it!" He pulled a twenty out of his alligator skin wallet and exchanged it for the two drinks. "Especially Crystal. What a hot mess! Didn't you love the comment Kate made about prostitutes wearing 'hot crotch pants'? I couldn't tell if she meant hot pants or crotchless panties!"

"I think she meant low-rise jeans," giggled Gemma.

"I need to bring that woman into the twenty-first century," Clark moaned. "Talk to you later?"

Gemma nodded as Clark bounced back to a group of APs. "This doesn't feel like much of a celebration without James," Gemma moped, turning back to the bar. "It was *his* show."

"Sorry," Dana shrugged, motioning for the bartender to pour another shot of Cuervo. She licked a dollop of salt off her wrist and pounded the tequila with a shudder. Obviously Dana was in no mood to console.

Gemma sighed, grabbing two vodka and Diet Cokes off the bar, and smiled at a few KMers as she made her way through the sticky, strobe-lit dance floor. RubyBar was trashy as hell. Even so, Gemma felt like quite the sassy little diva to be there.

"This doesn't seem like work," America remarked as Gemma sat down. America wouldn't know work if it jumped up and bit her on the trust fund, but she had a point. Body shots and table dancing hardly deserved a paycheck.

Gemma giggled, pleased that she was finally able to spot America's dry wit. Took her long enough. "Oh, yeah. It's just like this," she drawled, gesturing vaguely.

America rolled her eyes and clinked Gemma's glass before sipping her vodka and Diet Coke disdainfully. Yuck. America was usually a martini gal, but the perky RubyBar bartender didn't inspire much confidence.

"Thanks for leaving *me* to pay for the drinks," Dana moaned, slamming the table. Gemma opened her mouth to apologize but Dana zipped her. "Guess what fish I just spotted?" "Fish" was Dana-speak for celebrity: a fish in a bowl is always on display.

The girls bobbed their heads to Sean Paul and followed Dana's gaze. It was hard to see beyond the debaucherous KMers, but leaning against the wall in ripped jeans and a faded KISS T-shirt was an eerily familiar hottie with buzzed blonde hair and scruffy five o'clock shadow. He was all good looks and bad attitude, but Gemma couldn't place him and America didn't give a shit anyway.

"It's Kevin Donnelly," Dana said simply. Were they blind? "He's an actor—too hot and too dumb for anything else. Come on, let's go say hi!"

"You *know* him?" Gemma gasped, tripping as Dana pulled her up from the table.

"Who, *Dana*? Know a *celebrity*? Imagine," America deadpanned. She waved goodbye, opting to mope at their table and finish her drink.

Apparently Danny still hadn't returned her calls.

"A couple years ago, Kevin did a pilot with my step-bitch," Dana explained as they drew closer. "It was a horrible show and it ultimately drove Stepbitch into early retirement, but Kevin's up-and-coming. Haven't you seen *Finding Mr. Mann?*"

Of course, Gemma nodded. Kevin Donnelly played the soft-spoken high school jock on the CW drama *Finding Mr. Mann*. The show was sucktastic, but even Gemma knew Kevin's character was going through a major steroid story-line. It was quite the to-do.

"Kevy-Kev!" Dana cooed, sauntering up to him. "How have you been?" She kissed his right cheek and then his left, letting her moist lips linger.

"Well, if it isn't Dana Cox," Kevin murmured. His voice was as deep as the Marlboro Man and he looked just as good. Mmm. Gemma bit her lip wondering why she wasn't a bigger *Mr. Mann* fan. He wrapped his arms around Dana's waist and shook his head wickedly. "Lookin' *good*. Where you been?"

"My wicked stepmother keeps shipping me off to board-ing school. But you're in luck," Dana winked. She eased forward, inviting Kevin to check out the goods in her snug, black Ella Moss dress. "I'm staying in the city for my senior year."

Kevin smiled, rolling the neck of his beer against his lips. "Does Reese know about this?" he asked. He took a swig and tipped the bottle toward Dana.

"The stepbitch knows," Dana said. She grabbed the beer and pounded half of it without taking her eyes off

Kevin. "She's not too thrilled, but I've got a lot of money that says I'm going to Dillinger."

Kevin raised his eyebrows in approval. "Dillinger? I'm impressed," he said. "You know I filmed that pilot with Reese during my senior year at Dillinger."

Everybody knew that, but Dana nodded impressively like she didn't.

"Well, if I'm going to be an actress I need the best performing arts school."

"Maybe I can give you some *tips*," Kevin murmured lecherously.

Don't mind me, Gemma squirmed.

"Kevin, you're a slut," Dana teased. "What are you doing here anyway? This place is a pit."

"Research for my character," Kevin said, taking his beer back from Dana. "The steroids thing is going to spiral into alcoholism." He took another swig and nodded his head to the beat. "You should stop by the set. We're filming season two in Brooklyn."

"Didn't I read about that on *Page Six*?" America asked, appearing with a glass of merlot. Fame was beneath her but she had a weakness for the gossip section of *The New York Post*. She set her wine glass on an empty table beside them and adjusted the spaghetti straps of her Prada slip dress, extending her hand to Kevin. "America Vanderbilt."

Somehow when America introduced herself she made it sound like a national holiday. Not many people can pull off the gravitas of Joseph Stalin with the grace of Audrey Hepburn. Gemma for instance. It was possible Kevin hadn't even noticed her yet. *Sigh*. She sipped her drink, apathetically scanning the room. Would anyone be impressed that she was schmoozing with a TV star? Anyone *other* than the ubiquitous twins? They were so pathetically blatant. Anita's eyes were glued to Kevin Donnelly's ass and Maria was practically drooling. Gemma quickly turned back to her friends but it was too late. The piranhas had made eye contact.

"Hi Gemma!" Anita chirped, trotting up and kissing Gemma on the cheek. Suddenly they were BFF? Gag. "Who's your friend?"

"You met Dana at the party last weekend," Gemma said innocently. She so enjoyed watching them squirm.

"Duh," Maria groaned. "We mean your *other* friend." She batted her eyelashes and nibbled a sliver of pineapple from her piña colada.

Gemma smiled meekly. Was she allowed to introduce someone she hadn't technically been introduced to herself? Surely Emily Post had rules about that sort of thing.

"I'm Kevin," Kevin obliged with a slinky smile.

Anita giggled and whispered something in Maria's ear. Ugh. Were they five? Gemma was mortified. She *already* felt like an extra on *Degrassi* without the twins dragging her down. She sipped her drink thirstily, watching in disgust as they panted for Kevin Donnelly. And what was up with those ruffly black milkmaid outfits? Gemma didn't have to shop at Barney's to know that the Harajuku look was over.

"That's hilarious!" Maria giggled.

That's hilarious, Gemma mimicked, itching under her bra strap. Kevin was regaling them with *Mr. Mann* anecdotes.

They were driving Gemma crazy, but the twins were all five-karat-diamond-studded ears. Thrusting her weight from her right hip to her left, Gemma locked eyes with America and the two exchanged an exasperated eye roll. No wonder America was so down on the celebrity Tilt-a-Whirl. Kevin Donnelly may as well have been behind glass.

Suddenly Gemma's eyes bulged à la some deranged mad scientist. The line between brilliance and madness is blurry after tequila shots and a vodka Diet Coke, but Gemma was pretty sure there was an idea forming in her pretty little head. She pulled her cell phone out of her bag and furtively typed *Follow my lead*, then sent the text to Dana.

"You're right, Kevin," Gemma ad-libbed. "Maria and Anita have amazing presence."

Kevin looked at Gemma like she'd just asked him for a lap dance. Celebrities take misquotes *so* seriously.

"Really?" Maria gushed. She stuck out her chest and flashed Kevin smoldering bedroom eyes. "I get that a lot."

The corners of Kevin's mouth crinkled hesitantly. Whatever the plan was, it wasn't working and Gemma's window of opportunity was slamming shut. She bit her lip, flaring her eyeballs desperately at her friends.

"Yeah," Dana agreed vaguely. Like any C-list celebrity worth her salt, Dana had checked the text message instantly and was doing her best to follow Gemma's lead.

"And Kevin, didn't you say the CW's casting twins for a new story arc?" Gemma added. Nobody said anything and Gemma's palms began to sweat. This was a disaster. Dana was clueless, America was even *more* clueless, and Kevin couldn't care less. Gemma downed the rest of her vodka Diet Coke and liquid courage took over. "Too bad, though. With everything you guys have been through lately, it'd be hard to find representation."

"What's that supposed to mean?" Maria scoffed, crossing her arms.

"*You* know," Gemma answered suggestively. She leaned closer to the twin and stage-whispered, "The *harassment* suit."

"That's right!" Ding. Dana got it. "Gemma told us what happened..." She paused, frowning with concern, and turned to Kevin. "Their boss, you know, *tried something* with them."

"That sucks," Kevin said, pounding the rest of his beer.

"Yeah," Maria shrugged. "But we'd love to be on your show." She sipped her piña colada, seductively biting the straw for Kevin's benefit.

"Are you sure you're *ready* for that?" America asked with just a hint of condescension. Gemma smiled, grateful to have the world-weary wit of America Vanderbilt on her side.

Anita opened her mouth to speak but Dana was quicker. "Even if you weren't traumatized for life, I doubt you'll find an agent." Her voice lowered a bit as a Nelly Furtado song came to an end. "My stepmom's agent was always really picky about clients with *personal* problems," she said disdainfully. With a sharp elbow, she rammed Kevin in the ribs and he let out a startled cough.

"Right," Kevin nodded, fondling his ribs delicately. "It's a liability. Nobody decent would represent a loose wire. Look what happened to Tara Reid." He sighed, letting the hint of a smile creep onto his lips. "Too bad, though. I'm really getting into the idea of twins."

Anita and Maria glanced at each other, doing a quick twin-telepathy thing. Gemma couldn't help smiling. She *so* had them.

"It really wasn't that serious," Maria backpedaled. She was buckling. Even her lustrous tropical tan was wavering.

"No, but that sucks," Dana said, completely ignoring Maria's retraction. "Twins are *so* hot right now. And can you imagine getting to lock lips with Kevin? God, I'd clone myself to get that part!"

"Yeah," Kevin nodded enthusiastically. The typical male fantasy had taken over his brain.

Gemma held her breath. It was now or never. The twins had finished their telepathic conference call and one of them was about to erupt. She bit the tip of her thumbnail expectantly. It was like watching a jack-in-the-box.

More like excited puppies—five bucks says one of them pees on the floor.

"Nothing happened!" Anita blurted.

Gemma's jaws dropped like there was a five-pound weight attached. She was speechless. Seriously, how often does a harebrained scheme *actually* pan out?

"I swear," Anita went on, fueled by Kevin's stunned interest. "The whole thing was a joke."

"Anita!" Maria screamed. "What the fuck are you doing?"

As *Desperate Housewives* as this moment was, it was hard not to feel bad for Anita. Her wide, starved-for-attention eyes gleamed with hatred as she stood up to her twin for the first time in, well, probably *ever*. The tension was almost unbearable. A few KMers swiveled around, quickly sensing a massive pile of poo about to hit the fan.

"I'm not missing my fifteen minutes so you can keep up some lie," Anita yelled. "So you got James fired. So fucking what? Dad still ignores us, only now you're even more of a bitch." She paused for a breath, and a few more staffers turned to ogle the train wreck in progress. "But I'm going to be an *act*ress! Right Kevin?"

Poor, dumbstruck Kevin. All he wanted was a beer at a dive bar and he got some spazzed-out Britney circa the buzz cut.

Dana whistled a sigh, breaking the awkward silence. "Damn. That's some messed up shit to pull just to get attention. I'm impressed!"

"Very *Jerry Springer*," America added, cradling her glass of boxed wine with condemning superiority.

Maria opened her mouth to retort but Gemma put a finger to her bubble lips, savoring the moment. She'd been dreaming of this since the dreaded Nokia fiasco. Payback's a bitch, biatch!

"Don't," Gemma said in disgust. "In fact, why don't you guys just leave."

Anita gasped, turning red with shame, and scampered away like a subway rat. It was priceless. Everyone turned to Maria, eager to see what she'd do. Nothing, apparently, though for a minute Gemma thought they might have to rumble. Finally, with a crisp smile, Maria spun on her Miu Miu heels and strutted through the crowd of dumbstruck staffers.

"Well, well, well," America applauded as Maria vanished. "If it isn't our own little Lois Lane. How did you know they were lying?"

"Hoped against hope," Gemma smiled. She grabbed her empty glass off the table and chomped on a few ice cubes. Vindication made her thirsty.

"That was ... really ..." Kevin started to laugh. He wasn't much for the unscripted words. "Intense. Who wants to smoke a J in my car?"

"No thanks," Gemma giggled. She was already thirsty and she didn't need to add munchies to the mix.

America shook her head politely, too. She'd done the whole pot *thing* last summer. Dana, on the other hand, smiled wickedly at Kevin. She laced her fingers through his and led him out through a side door.

"Guess we're not going home with *her*," America sneered. "I'm going to try calling Danny again. Meet me outside in five?"

"Sure," Gemma nodded. She slung her purse over her shoulder and walked through the dance floor, still reeling from her own brilliance.

"Gemma, that was amazing!" Kamara cooed, squeezing Gemma's shoulder. "We all saw the twins' little psycho confession. I hope they fry!" She gave Gemma a high-five and danced back to Carla and Val.

A chill went up Gemma's spine as she continued through the dance floor. Thank god so many people had witnessed the whole mess. Now the story just had to trickle through the grapevine and back to Penelope O'Shea...

Gemma squeezed past Enid's ode-to-Flashdance and edged off the dance floor, slamming right into Nick. Shit. She stumbled to catch her balance and Nick caught her arm, just like he'd done the night of his party. He smiled lasciviously and Gemma shuddered, yanking her arm away from him.

"We've got to stop meeting like this," Nick slurred, kissing her cheek with slobbery lips. He smelled like tequila and he looked like the worm at the bottom of the bottle. "Can I buy you a drink?"

Gemma smiled, weighing her options. She could make fun of his spray-on tan. Or clue him in to the fact that metrosexual really *does* mean gay. Or she could tell him what a repulsive kisser he was. But Gemma was feeling frisky. She smiled girlishly and rested her hands on his shoulders. *Pull and thrust!*

Gemma cackled. It probably made her look like some psycho man-hater, but she couldn't help it. She'd never kneed a guy in the balls before. Well, she'd never known a guy who deserved it. But Nick definitely did, and it was invigorating.

Not to mention, a thousand times better than stolen champagne and *Scarface*—which was awesome, by the way.

As she turned to strut off the dance floor a few girls from the office whistled and applauded her. Apparently, Gemma wasn't the first girl to get slimed by Nick. She probably wouldn't be the last, either. But at least now he knew what the consequences were.

Ouch. The consequences were gonna need an ice pack.

TWENTY-FOUR

Gemma held the sizzling hot ceramic straightener to her hair and watched her frizzy locks form a paper-thin sheath around her head. "What do you wear when you're going to see the guy you want to spend the rest of your life with?"

Gemma was a *liiittle* overzealous about going to hear Subway Guy's band play.

"Hmm." Dana cocked her head thoughtfully as she applied M.A.C. lipstick in Hue. "Something that's easy to take off?" she answered wickedly.

"Very helpful, Trampy McWhore." America jabbed Dana's elbow with her shoulder, somewhat accidentally causing the lipstick to glide off Dana's plump lips and onto her cheek. Very Bozo the Epileptic Clown.

"Bitch!" Dana gasped, giggling at the nude lightning bolt across her face. She scanned her white marble bathroom for a weapon of retaliation and settled on a tub of Hard Candy body glitter. "Take that!" she giggled, blowing its sparkly golden contents all over America's sleek black Gucci dress.

America's jaw dropped as she looked down at what used to be a five-thousand-dollar silk strapless dress. That was going to be a bitch to clean. Her eyes zeroed in on a bottle of mousse and she lunged for it.

"Truce, you guys!" Gemma yelped, hurling her body between America and the hair product. She wasn't about to let some glammed-out catfight hinder her pseudo-date with the most perfect man alive.

Way to keep the expectations low.

With a ragged sigh, she handed Dana a Ponds facial wipe and grabbed the hair dryer to deglitter America. Then she took a step back, admiring her reflection in a flower-print strapless Tibi dress. Miss Moneybags Vanderbilt bought it on sale, so Gemma *had* to wear it. The fact that it fit like a glove didn't hurt, either. She tightened the white leather belt, hoping Joe would like it as much as she did.

"He's gonna love you, Gem," Dana answered telepathically. She scrutinized her own reflection, tackling the lipstick stain with warm soapy water. "Besides, once I tell him you're a Mean-Green-Ball-Busting-Machine he'll be too scared to say otherwise."

"Thanks ... *Mrs. Donnelly!*" Gemma giggled, turning back to the hair straightener.

Dana rolled her eyes. She'd been called a lot worse. But that didn't change the fact that she'd been with Kevin Donnelly all night in the back of his limo.

"So Gemma. What's the news on those crafty little twins?" America asked, finally shutting off the hair dryer. The few remaining sparkles looked intentional and fabulous.

"I don't know," Gemma frowned. "People were definitely talking about them at work today, but I didn't even see them. I wonder if Ms. O'Shea found out. Maybe she'll even give James his job back!"

"Gemma," America hesitated before pressing a soft cocoa liner to her lips. "Why are you such a cheerleader for this James guy?"

Gemma put the hair straightener on the counter and bent down, fiddling with the buckles on her Mary Janes. *Cheerleader?* she huffed. There were a couple reasons she'd helped, but being someone's cheerleader was *not* one of them.

"Because of Anita and Maria," Gemma answered finally. "Those girls have been screwing me since day one and I want them to suffer." She stepped into a cloud of Stella McCartney perfume and wiggled around. "That's the superficial, catty reason. The other reason, however lame it sounds, is that James is a good guy and everyone just gave up on him. It drives me friggin' crazy how jaded everyone is. I can't take it!"

"Amen, sista!" Dana cheered. She pulled a beaded antique hoop through her ear and stubbed her cigarette out in a silver monogrammed ashtray by the sink. "Let's motor."

The girls grabbed their clutch bags—complete with fake IDs, credit cards, perfume, and lipstick—and sauntered into the hot evening air to hail a cab. Gemma stared out the window as they sped down Columbus Avenue, completely freaking out about seeing Joe ... and introducing him to her friends ... and what they'd think of him ... and what she'd say to him ... and what he'd say to her ...

Blah, blah, blah. Can a person die from over-hypothesizing?

"This is it," the cabby grumbled.

Gemma eased onto Ludlow Street, suddenly flashing back to their crazy night at Slip. Had it really been two weeks ago? So much had happened since then, but Gemma still felt awkward as hell going to a club. Lucky for her there were no bouncers or glitterati to impress this time. She took a shaky breath and followed Dana down a steep, dimly lit set of stairs into a basement bar. The place was moderately packed for ten p.m. on a Thursday, but as far as Gemma could tell there was no band set up. There was barely even *room* for a band. Still, the girls wandered in, grabbing the first empty banquette they saw.

"This place is phat," Dana decided. She grabbed her bedazzled money clip and pointed toward the bar. "First round's on me. Orders?"

"Cosmopolitan?" Gemma said as her eyes flitted nervously around the room.

"What the hell," America agreed with a wave. She picked a speck of glitter off her bare shoulder and surveyed the room, yawning slightly. Hipster-chic was *not* her scene. Any other night she would have hightailed it out of there, but Gemma looked so pathetically desperate. America felt sorry for the little cornhusker and wanted to be supportive.

"This place is cool, right?" Gemma said hopefully. She *so* wanted it to be cool.

"Holy shit," Dana panted, reappearing out of nowhere. "You are never going to believe who I just saw."

Both girls shrugged. If it wasn't Joe, Gemma didn't care, and unless it was Danny, neither did America.

Dana huffed and squatted next to Gemma. "It's my DJ. The one that laughed at me!" She swiveled her head to the left and pointed to a DJ booth in the next room.

"What an asshole," America said, squinting. The room was too dark to get a good look. "But—" She stopped, noticing the wheels spinning round and round in Dana's frizzy blonde head. "You're not going to do something stupid, are you? You haven't made it into the tabloids yet this summer. Shouldn't we try and keep it that way?" She squeezed Dana's hand and tapped her Balenciaga pump against the floor. Where was her goddamn Cosmo already? "Why don't I get the drinks."

"No. I'll do it," Dana said, regaining her composure. She stood up tall and adjusted her skimpy Heatherette top. "I want him to see what he's missing."

"Can you believe her?" America sighed as Dana tore a path of destruction toward the bar. "I love that girl, but bitch knows how to hold a grudge."

Gemma nodded vaguely, unable to take her eyes off the DJ booth. Daft Punk morphed into Stereolab and she blinked, wondering if there was any possibility that this was *not* happening. Oh, but it was. In the next room over, spinning a dizzying electronic beat, stood Joe "Subway Guy" Cross.

What are the odds?

"Gemma," America said, waving her hand in front of Gemma's face. "You look like you've seen Star Jones naked. Are you okay?"

The room started to spin and Gemma choked. Was she a total idiot for not putting two and two together? Please. Like she could have known that out of a billion New Yorkers she and Dana were crushing on the same one.

But suddenly the similarities were exploding in Gemma's head like fireworks: They both had brown hair; brown eyes; the DJ/musician thing; even his name—Dana thought the DJ's name was Jon, right?

Of course it was all a coincidence, but Gemma was being overdramatic, as usual.

"I'm a horrible person!" Gemma wailed to America. She covered her face with her hands and mumbled, "That's Joe."

"What? Where!" Dana asked, reappearing out of nowhere, balancing three Cosmos between her hands. She doled out the drinks and scootched into the booth, keenly eyeing the crowd for the infamous Joe.

Gemma bit her lip, wondering what she'd done to deserve this. Had she been a pedophile in a former life or something? She smiled nervously at Dana and picked up her bright pink Cosmo with both hands.

"Well?" Dana asked.

"I'm going to the bathroom," America blurted out. She liked Gemma and all, but she hadn't signed on for this. The cornhusker was on her own.

Gemma brought the Cosmo to her lips and gulped half of it down. Cottonmouth was killing her but the vodka burned her throat into oblivion. Her face reddened from the lack of oxygen. She gasped for air, waving away Dana's offer to help and looked toward the DJ booth. Why was it *empty*? And where the hell was Joe? Gemma had to act fast.

"Dana," she choked. "I have to tell you something. You know that guy—"

"Gemma?"

Too late.

"It's brilliant that you made it," Joe smiled, taking Gemma's hand. He wasn't the most gorgeous guy in the room but there was something adorkable about him. And there were at least five girls in the bar glaring at Gemma for nabbing him—including one pissed-as-hell Dana.

"I'm really chuffed to see you," Joe continued obliviously. "You look smashing. Really gorgeous."

It was almost too painful to watch.

With an uncomfortable smile, Gemma wriggled free from Joe's tender grasp and shoved her hand in her lap. How could she enjoy this while Dana's demon eyes were burning a hole in her head? She knew she had to say something, but what? *Sorry I stole your boyfriend even though he likes me and he wasn't yours to begin with?*

Yeah. That'd go over well.

"I'm leaving," Dana seethed through gritted teeth. She stood up and knocked back her Cosmo in one gulp. Then she wiped her mouth with the back of her hand and brushed past them, shooting Gemma the world's evilest glare.

"Oh god," Gemma sighed, resting her head in her hands. She felt like the scum of the universe. Tears welled up in her eyes as she feebly pushed herself up from the table. "I have to ... I have to go," she whispered.

She couldn't let Dana run off thinking that she'd stolen her guy.

"What happened?" America asked, strutting up to the table. "Where's Dana?"

Gemma shook her head, barely able to hold back the tears. The three of them stood there quietly in varying levels of confusion until Joe cleared his throat. He looked *beyond* puzzled.

"Gemma?" he asked softly. He shoved his hands in his pockets and looked around the room. For a hidden camera, perhaps?

"I have to go," Gemma said again, grabbing her purse. She stumbled up the steps and onto the street, bursting into tears. Dana was gone. Gemma stomped her Mary Janes against the pavement. She couldn't believe this was happening to her. Joe was supposed to be an adorable English rocker, not Dana's asshole DJ.

"So that was Joe," America observed, catching up to Gemma on the sidewalk. "He's cute."

Gemma sniffled and wiped a tear off her cheek.

"What happened?"

"I was about to tell her," Gemma swore. She limped down the sidewalk aimlessly. "I started choking on my drink like a loser and by the time I stopped, Joe was standing next to me. He said all this stuff that would have been really sweet if..."

Sob.

America patted Gemma on the back. "It's not your fault." She walked to the edge of the street and waved down a taxi. "You didn't know it was the same guy... right?"

"Of *course* not!" Gemma yelped, scurrying after America. "I would never do that to her. God, I'm such an idiot," she moaned.

"There, there," America consoled somewhat insincerely. She pushed Gemma into the cab and handed the driver a fifty. "Eighty-Third and CPW, *now!*"

BACK TALK

"Antes de morir..."

Gemma and America walked into the house and followed voices upstairs to the casual living room where Dana and Gabriella sat curled up on the sofa drinking tea and avidly watching cheesy Mexican soaps.

"Antes de morir..." the woman choked. She was lying in the middle of the desert with a nasty gunshot wound. It didn't look good for her, but Gemma would have gladly traded places with the woman. *"Yo quiero ver..."*

America cleared her throat, but Dana made no effort to acknowledge their presence. Yup, definitely still mad. The girls walked in farther and eased onto the opposite sofa, smiling awkwardly at Gabriella. Gemma gulped. Having a fight in front of the mild-mannered housekeeper was going to be extremely unpleasant.

America cleared her throat again. "I think this has—"

"Gabby and I are watching *Gitanas*," Dana snapped. "Could you leave us alone?"

"What are you yelling at me for?" America pouted, grabbing a mint off the coffee table. She leaned back and turned her attention to the TV, unintentionally getting sucked in to the dying woman's last request to see her long lost son, brother, or husband—it was hard to tell.

Gemma hovered on the edge of her seat, debating whether to run up to her room and cry or run to the bathroom and puke. Fighting made her nauseous. She stared at Dana, desperate to get her attention, but Queen Grudgeholder was having none of it. Damn. The woman showed no mercy!

Gemma couldn't take it anymore. She cupped her hand over her mouth and hauled ass to the third floor guest bathroom. At first she just dry heaved over the toilet, but then up came her Cosmopolitan and then a cheese enchilada. Tasty. She flushed the toilet and staggered to the mirror, wincing at her reflection. Mascara streaks, swollen cheeks. Tammy Faye, eat your heart out.

"*And* I smell like puke," Gemma snickered mournfully. Icing on the cake.

"Gemma?" America said, tapping her knuckles against the door. "You okay?"

Gemma didn't answer. Instead she turned on the faucet and splashed her face over and over again, wondering how long she could barricade herself in there. Not long enough.

Reluctantly she shut off the water and dried her face, leaving a splotchy trail of mascara on the pristine Ralph Lauren hand towel. Oops. She laughed dismally, wishing she could just flush herself down the toilet and be done with it.

"Dana, you must listen to her." Gabriella was on the other side of the door now, too, and she sounded stern. "Gemma is your friend. You see her in pain and you still angry at her? I am ashamed."

There was a pause. Gemma pressed her ear to the door, waiting for a cease-fire. Then Gabriella sighed heavily and shuffled downstairs. *Damn*, Gemma sighed. Gabby was her only ally. On the count of three, she opened the bathroom door and followed voices down the hall to Dana's room. Both her friends were sitting on Dana's bed with folded arms and sullen faces. Super.

"You're such a bitch," Dana grunted, hugging a pillow to her chest. "How could you do that to me?"

Ugh. If everyone took fights this seriously we'd still be in the middle of the Trojan fucking War.

"I swear I didn't know," Gemma whimpered. She waited in vain for a response but Dana's poker face was impenetrable. "You barely told us anything about that guy and that was three weeks ago. You could have at least said he was English. That *might* have narrowed the field a *little*."

"It was really loud when I met him," Dana pouted. "And when he laughed at me? Well, that's pretty fucking universal. But come on, Gemma. You did this on purpose."

"Are you crazy?" Gemma shrieked. "I would never do that to you." She scanned Dana's floor and reached for the new *Vogue*. Sitting up tall, Gemma placed one hand on *Vogue* and the other in the air. "I swear on"—she peeked down at the cover—"Gwyneth Paltrow: I had no idea my guy was your guy."

Dana snatched *Vogue* out of Gemma's hands and volunteered a lopsided smile. "Fine," she huffed sarcastically. "I just freaked out when I saw you with him. Especially after he laughed at me. Even my therapist doesn't know what to do with that."

America rolled her eyes.

"I'm serious!" Dana giggled. "God. I'm as neurotic as Gemma, aren't I?"

"Hey!" Gemma laughed defensively. She hopped on the bed and put her head in Dana's lap. "I can't believe he laughed at you. That's so un-Joe-like."

"Maybe if Danny was here, he'd know..."

The Danny pedestal was reaching new heights.

Gemma and Dana looked at America with puppy dog eyes.

"What?" America said innocently.

"Come here." Dana pulled America in for a bear hug and added a free noogie. "You'll work things out with Danny. He finally called you back, right?"

America nodded, trying to smooth down her natty hair.

"Look at Gemma and me," Dana added dismally. "We're fighting over some dude I didn't even know was English."

Gemma laughed miserably. "At least you've got your CW hottie, right?"

"True," Dana nodded with a wicked grin. "I can't wait till the stepbitch finds out. She'll die!"

The girls laughed but Gemma could feel the inevitable "poor me" lump forming in her throat. Dana had her hunky movie star, America was probably planning a romantic rendezvous to Japan, and all Gemma had was fat thighs and no Joe. She held her breath to stop from crying, but it was useless.

"I don't understand," Gemma wailed. "He was so sweet when we had coffee."

"I know," Dana said soothingly. She combed Gemma's ironed hair with her fingers and sighed. "Maybe you should give him another chance."

"What?" America asked. "Did you eat a brain tumor for breakfast?"

There she goes again with the *Heathers* quotes.

"Ten seconds ago you were about to boil Gemma's bunny rabbit and now you're telling her to go for it?"

"Danny gave *you* a second chance, didn't he?" Dana argued. "Besides, as much as it made me want to *gag*, Joe looked at Gemma like the sun shines out of her ass."

"Nicely put, Emily Dickinson."

Gemma smiled in a doe-eyed stupor.

"Did he ... *really*?"

TWENTY-FIVE

"'Scuse me," Gemma moaned, fighting her way across Broadway through a herd of gawking tourists. She dashed across the street as the light flicked from yellow to red and turned east onto Fifty-Seventh Street.

"Hey Gemma!" Clark yelled from a coffee kiosk on the corner. Gemma ran up and kissed him on the cheek, and they continued briskly along Fifty-Seventh. "I'm still reeling over that crap you pulled on Nick." Clark chuckled, pausing for a sip of coffee. "You're *so Alias* these days. God, remember when you got here a month ago? Young, innocent, shy—not even sassy enough to mix stripes with solids. But look at you now!"

Gemma giggled humbly as they crossed Seventh Ave.

"I always knew there was something sketch about that *Nick* character."

Clark said "Nick" the way he might say Osama Bin Laden or Celine Dion.

"As if!" Gemma cried. "You were practically begging me to—"

"Gemma!"

Both Clark and Gemma swiveled toward the desperate voice coming from behind them. It was Crystal. Clark's jaw dropped and Gemma slapped her hand to her mouth as Crystal inched toward them. She was standing in the street in a torn white tank top and dirty denim shorts. The girl looked like death warmed over.

"Oh my god," Gemma gasped, wondering where on earth she'd appeared from. "Crystal, are you okay?"

"I'll ... see you later," Clark murmured. He knew a train wreck when he saw one.

Gemma yanked Crystal onto the sidewalk and pulled a bottle of water out of her bag. "Drink this. What are you doing here? Why aren't you under protective custody?"

Crystal pounded the water and tossed the empty bottle into the gutter. She took a step closer to Gemma and threw her arms in the air. "You tell me, bitch!"

Whoa. Gemma's eyes widened. What happened to happy, grateful Crystal on her way to boarding school in Albany? And how did she get so freakin' dirty?

"Calm down, Crystal. I don't know what you're—"

"Bullshit," Crystal spat. Gemma blushed as onlookers gathered around them, but Crystal was oblivious. "I been calling Carla all morning. Bitch put me on hold for fifteen minutes then hung up. You think you can chuck me in some skanked-out homeless shelter and forget about me? What kind of scam are y'all pulling?"

Scam? What was she talking about? Gemma put her hand on Crystal's bony shoulder and tried to shush her. "Please, just tell me what happened."

Crystal brushed Gemma's hand away and leaned against a Nine West display window, letting her body sink down to the sidewalk. Then she looked up expectantly. Gemma hesitated, then crouched awkwardly beside her.

"It's Kenny. He's out."

"Out?" Gemma choked. "What do you mean 'out'? 'Out' as in 'out of jail'?" It never happened that fast on *Law & Order.*

"He's looking for me," Crystal whimpered, scanning the streets frantically. "And when he finds me, I'm dead."

Gemma shook her head in disbelief and pulled her brown waves into a banana clip. Since when was she Crystal's fairy godmother? She rummaged around in her bag and handed a rumpled but clean tissue to Crystal.

"Come on." Gemma stood, pulling Crystal up with her. "I'm taking you up to the office. Timothy will know what to do."

A hollow, sinking sensation festered inside Gemma as she realized, a little too late, that this had been a bad idea. Timothy wanted to help Crystal like he wanted a bubble bath in burning hot lava. His plasticine smile said it all.

"Crystal!" Timothy cooed through clenched teeth. "Would you excuse us for a sec?" He pushed her into the hallway, slamming the door in her frightened, dirty face and turned to Gemma. "What the hell is she doing here?"

Gemma bit her thumbnail, staring at Timothy in his snazzy Juicy Couture blazer and pressed ivory chinos. Was she on crack? Of course he didn't give a flying nun about Crystal Bloom. The framed picture of himself on his desk implied other interests. But that couldn't stop Gemma. She was incensed. Timothy and his *outfit* were going to have to deal. She took a deep breath and let it rip. Consequences be damned.

"We have to do something," Gemma boomed, practically jumping at the authority in her voice. Even Timothy blinked in shock. "Crystal's pimp got out on bail and he's going to come after her. And did you know we put her up in some filthy, half-assed homeless shelter with no security?"

Timothy feigned surprise as he plucked a cat hair off his yellow collared shirt.

"Crystal risked her life to be on this show," Gemma roared, thrusting her finger in his pointy little face. "How can you just throw her away like a piece of trash? I mean, her pimp wants to *kill* her. Can you honestly live with the blood of a thirteen-year-old girl on your hands?"

Overdramatic much?

Timothy thrust his hands onto his hips and huffed like a Valley Girl. "Excuse me?" He chuckled self-righteously. "How dare you talk to me like that. You are *so* fired."

Gemma gulped, suddenly plummeting back down to Earth. What was she doing? Of course butting heads with a producer would get her fired. She took a step back, wondering how she'd gone from human rights advocate to fired. Was Crystal really worth all this? Rubbing her temples methodically, Gemma glanced over her shoulder through Timothy's floor-to-ceiling window overlooking the hallway.

Crystal stared back at her. She must have heard them. The *Back Talk* offices were hardly soundproof. Gemma sighed. Her decision was made. And yes, she'd probably get fired, but it didn't matter. Slowly, she opened the door and walked out into the hallway.

"Hold on a sec, Crystal." Gemma smiled nervously and walked down the hall. The large, oak door leading into the executive producer's office was closed, but Gemma held her breath and knocked.

After a moment, a muffled voice replied, "Yes?"

With a shaky breath, Gemma gently pushed the door open and peeked her head in. "Ms. O'Shea?"

The slender redhead looked up from *Hello* magazine. "Yes?"

"Hi." Gemma's voice cracked. "I need to talk to you. Actually, I need you to come with me. It's about Crystal Bloom—the prostitute from the show the other day?"

Ms. O'Shea frowned in confusion and studied Gemma for a moment. "Well, all right." She hesitated then rose to her feet, pulling a pink pashmina around her shoulders.

Gemma's heart thudded as the executive producer followed her down the hallway. A million thoughts were racing through her head, few of them resulting in her *not* getting fired.

"Ms. O'Shea, this is Crystal Bloom."

Crystal slouched in the chair she'd usurped and gave Penelope O'Shea the once over. "Who's she?"

Like a dog sensing fear, Timothy suddenly poked his head into the hallway. *Busted.* He shot Gemma a venomous scowl and smiled sheepishly at Ms. O'Shea. Silence. Everybody was waiting for somebody else to speak. Tick... tick... tick...

"Timothy?" Ms. O'Shea asked, bewildered. "Care to share?"

Timothy bobbed his head in submission and invited her into his office.

Commence fireworks.

Gemma and Crystal sat quietly outside the office, exchanging awkward smiles and uncomfortable laughter as Penelope O'Shea tore Timothy a new one. Ouch. The girls couldn't hear the conversation word for word, but there was a lot of scolding, a few expletives, and maybe even a little Gaelic. A small crowd of curious employees formed outside the office, none more curious than Gemma, who was 99.9 percent sure she'd be out of a job by lunchtime.

The eavesdroppers scattered like cockroaches as Ms. O'Shea finally emerged from Timothy's office fifteen minutes later with a harrowed smile on her face. She tugged at her shawl and bent down to Crystal.

"I'm so sorry about all this, darlin'," Ms. O'Shea said with genuine concern in her Irish voice. "We've straightened out this whole mess. I know a well-respected battered women's shelter on Long Island and I'm having one of Kate Morgan's bodyguards escort you there *personally*, right now."

In true Crystal fashion, Crystal just shrugged, but the girl looked visibly relieved.

"Awesome!" Gemma whooped. She jumped to her feet and wrapped Crystal in a bear hug. She might still get fired, but hey, at least justice had been served. "I'm so sorry," she added in a whisper.

With some force, Crystal wiggled out of Gemma's stifling embrace and took a step back. She shoved her hands in her dirty denim pockets and cleared her throat. The crowd had reformed, and Crystal looked skittish. "So can I go already?"

As if on cue, a tall Italian man in a black suit and dark shades appeared at the end of the hall.

"Parker will take you." Ms. O'Shea gingerly patted Crystal's matted hair and pushed her encouragingly toward Parker. "The shelter has very high security—nobody's going to find you there. And I've arranged for you to stay until August when the fall semester at Ramsey begins."

"Thanks," Crystal mumbled, looking down at her platform wedges. Slowly she turned, edging down the hall toward the expressionless bodyguard.

Gemma half expected Crystal to come running back, thanking her tearfully for going above and beyond the call of duty. But this wasn't a Disney movie, and Crystal wasn't Pollyanna. Sigh.

"Gemma."

A burst of fear coursed through Gemma's body as she turned. Penelope O'Shea was standing in front of her, poker-faced and rigid. Oh God. Gemma gulped audibly, searching for her voice. Damn. What she wouldn't give for an ally right now. But it sure as hell wasn't going to be Timothy. The smug little bastard looked like he wanted a box of popcorn.

"Could I see you in my office?" Ms. O'Shea said sharply. "Timothy, have Roger Kim join us there as well, please?"

Timothy nodded, his insufferably smug grin growing by the second. Roger Kim was the Executive in Charge of Production—not that Gemma knew what an EIC did. All that business/legal crap was way too boring to understand. Nonetheless, Roger Kim's invitation to the impromptu meeting probably meant one thing: Gemma go bye-bye.

"Take a seat," Ms. O'Shea prodded as they entered her luxurious corner office.

Gemma hovered by a coat rack, looking around the large room. There were wall-to-wall dry-erase boards covered in upcoming show notes and a section devoted to *Back Talk* newspaper clippings. In the far corner, a drool-worthy picture window overlooked the southern tip of Central Park. And gleaming gold and luminous atop a row of shelves sat Ms. O'Shea's prized Emmy award. The thing was probably hooked up to a silent alarm. Gemma lowered herself slowly onto a cold leather sofa and swallowed hard, trying not to throw up. The girl could throw up on a dime.

"Listen," Ms. O'Shea said, leaning against her desk. "Before Roger gets in here, I want to ..."

Fire you ... Ream you like I reamed Timothy ... Have you killed ...

"Commend you," she finished. "Crystal was falling through the cracks and you stepped up to the plate. That took backbone."

Backbone? Gemma marveled. That was a new one. She smiled inwardly as a short but gruff man pushed the door open.

"Oh, Gemma's here," Roger boomed in surprise as he slammed the door shut behind him. "Good." He grabbed a wooden armchair and dragged it toward the sofa, sitting opposite Gemma. Roger was a small man. The last name Kim would suggest Korean descent, but Roger looked pretty run-of-the-mill American. However slight his frame, it didn't change the fact that Gemma's fate rested in his hands.

"Here's the deal, Gemma," Ms. O'Shea began. She sat on the opposite end of the sofa and crossed her long legs, revealing a small rose tattoo on her left ankle. "We heard through the grapevine what happened the other night. With Maria and Anita Cruz."

Gemma's face reddened. It was about time somebody brought the twins up. She cleared her throat and focused on Ms. O'Shea's strawberry pink pashmina. Color therapy was hokey, but right now Gemma would try anything to stay calm.

"We were all upset to lose James," Ms. O'Shea continued. "But if the twins invented sexual harrassment charges ... well, that's serious."

"We heard *you* provoked the Cruz girls to recant," Roger butted in, leaning forward in his chair. "We'd like to hear the story from you. Care to elaborate?"

No pressure, Gemma gulped, rubbing her sweaty palms together in her lap. Roger sounded like an SAT administrator, and no, Gemma did not care to elaborate.

"Okay," Gemma began slowly. What to say, what to say ... "Well, I ... I had a feeling they were lying. And not like this is retribution or anything, but they planted that cell phone in my bag that first week. I swear. And—" Gemma bit her tongue. *Don't go overboard.* "I know Anita and Maria are ..." Spoiled brats? Teacher's pets? "Respected around the office, I just don't trust them. They're usually all over James, not the other way around."

Ms. O'Shea fiddled with the tassels on her pashmina and nodded.

"So, Wednesday night, they were drooling over this actor guy my friend Dana knows, and—"

"Reese Cox's daughter?" Ms. O'Shea interjected, smiling. "How is she?"

"Uh, fine?" Gemma replied with a shrug. Did the woman want to hear her story or not? "Anyway, we invented this story. Kevin pretended the girls were perfect for a role on his TV show, but Dana went on this rampage about girls with sexual abuse history not getting agents or something."

Roger Kim squinted, barely able to keep up, but Ms. O'Shea nodded, grinning at the tenacity of it all.

"After that it just came out," Gemma shrugged. *Like dirty laundry.* "Anita admitted the whole thing was a lie to get their father's attention. Actually," she tapped her chin thoughtfully, "it was pretty sad. Maria looked like she was going to kill her sister, but she didn't disagree or anything. After that they took off."

"Well, well, well," Ms. O'Shea hummed scandalously. "That's quite a yarn."

Gemma shrank down in her seat. Was that yarn about to spin her ass out of a job?

Ms. O'Shea exchanged a meaningful glance with Roger Kim, then looked back at Gemma with a doleful grin. "Of course, the Cruz girls denied everything." She paused long enough for Gemma to have a mini-coronary, finally adding, "but I think we've got a good idea of what *really* happened."

Five pounds of paranoia lifted off Gemma's shoulders. Finally they knew the truth. About frigging time. She looked back and forth at her two bosses, waiting impatiently. What next?

"It took a lot of guts to call them out," Roger added, crossing his legs. "It's hard to point fingers when it concerns the boss, or the boss's daughters, as the case may be." He paused briefly for a self-satisfying snicker. "But the *chutzpah* of those girls?"

Was that a rhetorical question?

Ms. O'Shea stood. "If things go well, James will be re-instated."

"Really?" Gemma smiled. This was *so* much better than getting fired. She rose to her feet and waved. "So, I guess I should get back to work now?" For a split second she thought about curtsying, but then remembered what decade it was and scurried out of the office.

She walked down the hallway, positively giddy. The twins were out and James *might* be back in. And to top it off, Gemma Winters had backbone.

Who knew?

TWENTY-SIX

Gemma hobbled up Columbus Avenue like Quasimodo in Manolos. Walking home from work seemed like such a stellar idea, but that was half an hour and three blisters ago and she was dying now. She fished around in her bag for cab fare. Ninety-three cents. Ninety-three cents would practically take her backwards. No thanks.

"Three more blocks," Gemma promised herself as she passed Starbucks. It may as well have been three thousand. She paused at a traffic light and gingerly eased her heel out of her pump. *Ahhh.*

"I know you're upset with me."

The soft English accent made Gemma's skin tingle. She turned slowly. It was Joe. And he looked as cute as ever in his typical button-down-shirt-with-sleeves-rolled-up, jeans, and Chuck Taylors. Gemma repressed a girlish grin and looked around. Where the hell had he come from? He must have been lurking around Starbucks waiting for her. Sneaky bastard.

"Just leave me alone," Gemma groaned, painfully jamming her foot back into her shoe. The light changed and she limped across Eighty-First Street.

"Please talk to me," Joe begged. He ran up ahead and walked backwards so they were face to face. Gemma was slower than a turtle in those heels. "At least tell me what I've done."

Like he didn't *know*. Well, actually he didn't.

Gemma harrumphed and brushed past him.

"Gemma," Joe pleaded again. He sounded so tortured. "I swear I'll leave you alone if you just tell me."

Gemma stopped on Eighty-Second and Columbus and put her hands on her hips. Fine. If it would get him off her back, she'd spell it out for him. "That was Dana sitting with me last night."

Nothing. Echo ... echo ...

"My best friend ... Dana Cox," Gemma elaborated. Un-*believ*able. "*Dana*, who gave you her number at Globe a few weeks ago?" If he didn't get it now he was just an idiot.

Still no response.

No. It took a second but the light bulb finally went on and Joe started to nod.

Gemma's heart fell. Like any love-struck fool, a part of her had hoped it was just a misunderstanding. But there was Joe, nodding and *getting* it. He knew exactly who Dana was, and therefore, he was exactly the cad she thought he was. What a bummer.

Joe flashed a sly grin. "You thought I was interested in your mate?"

Now he was grinning? What a pompous piece of—

"Wait," Joe said, putting his hand on Gemma's shoulder as she walked away. "Girls are handing me numbers all the time." He tripped on a crack in the pavement and slapped his forehead. "That came off really conceited, didn't it? But it's true. When I'm spinning at a club, it just happens, yeah? Usually all they're after is a snog—not that your mate was," he quickly added. Then he snickered, "Pickin' up birds on the tube is more my style."

Joe's irresistible charm wasn't going to work anymore. Gemma rolled her eyes and pushed past him, hightailing it up the street. Foot surgery was definitely in her immediate future, but she needed to make an exit.

"I had no idea your friend would get so upset," Joe yelled. "I thought she was just after a good time."

Yeah, like calling Dana a slut was *really* going to get him back in Gemma's good graces.

"Yeah, well she did get upset," Gemma said, turning onto Eighty-Third Street. "And that still doesn't explain why you laughed at her."

Another blank stare. Was she talking to a wall?

"Dana saw you in Soho a couple weeks ago," Gemma spat accusingly. "You and your friends laughed in her face. Explain *that*," she challenged.

"That was your mate?" Joe hooted. He pushed up his sleeves and shook with laughter. "Oh, that's awful. It had nothing to do with her, believe me. I was standing on the corner with a couple of my mates, yeah? And I was telling them about this girl I'd met." He paused. Gemma didn't get it. "I was telling them about *you*, Gemma."

Swoon. How could she keep up the cold shoulder Ice Queen act when Joe was so adorable? She slowed down, letting him walk next to her.

"Remember our chat about your prostitution story?"

Gemma nodded. She had no idea where Joe was going with this, but she was intrigued.

"You looked so frustrated," Joe continued. "I just wanted to help, yeah? Well, my mate Tom says 'Why don't we go and find a prostitute for her show.' And then I say 'Yeah, mate, but where are we going to find one? It's not as if they just walk up to you in the middle of the street.'"

"And *that's* when Dana walked up to you?" Gemma filled in. She was dubious to say the least, but his story was too absurd to be made up.

"Exactly," Joe said, clapping his hands together. "I know it was bad form to laugh, but you've got to admit it was funny. You believe me, right?" Joe asked, raising his eyebrows expectantly.

Gemma let out a heavy sigh, tugging at her faded denim skirt as she neared the apartment. She tilted her head and looked up at a cluster of wispy clouds. Of course she believed him, but he deserved to suffer for a minute. Women can be so cruel.

"I guess so," Gemma finally relented.

"You're gullible," Joe muttered. "Kidding! I'm kidding," he quickly added as Gemma's palm swung toward his cheek. He grabbed her hand and held it. "I think you're great, Gemma. I've liked you ever since I freaked you out on the subway. Remember that thing I said about Mother Nature?"

Gemma giggled. That was, like, a million years ago, but she remembered. She stopped in front of the apartment and leaned against the stoop. The sun was still blazing down on them but a slight evening breeze made it bearable. She couldn't believe how totally perfect this felt.

Yeah, perfect—layered with confusion and unnecessarily complicated, but perfect.

Joe leaned close to Gemma then pulled away awkwardly. "So you're not mad, then?"

Gemma shook her head breathlessly.

"Okay." He bit his lip and whispered, "In that case, could I kiss you?"

Only an Englishman would *ask* first. But Gemma had to admit it was devastatingly romantic.

Gemma gulped. In fantasyland, kissing Joe was this flawless, surreal experience, but this was real life. Her feet were throbbing, her stomach was in knots, and she had tuna breath. Nobody has tuna breath in a fantasy.

"Uh," she choked, but another voice boomed down from above.

"Kiss her, you loser!"

Gemma and Joe looked up to see Dana and America peeking their heads out of a second floor window. Again, not part of the fantasy. Gemma cradled her head in embarrassment as her friends passed a pair of binoculars back and forth.

"Recognize her now?" Gemma winced.

"Umm, yeah," Joe laughed. He wasn't nearly as mortified as Gemma but he had a little bit of a blush going on. "I guess you have to go."

Gemma forced a nod and started to walk up the stoop. Even if she did believe Joe's story, it probably made sense to run it by Dana first. That would be the *good friend* thing to do.

But nobody's good *all* the time.

Gemma spun around on her heels and flew down the steps, sliding her hand behind Joe's neck and gently pulling his lips to hers. It was like kissing a caramel. Joe wrapped his arms around her waist and Gemma melted. His story better be true, because he was a *really* amazing kisser.

Gemma pulled away when Dana started to whistle and applaud. Could she *be* any more annoying?

"Call me tomorrow?" Gemma asked. She grabbed a pen out of her bag and quickly wrote her number on the back of his hand then ran up the steps. She waved goodbye and ran into the house, slamming the door shut behind her. Dana and America were waiting for her on the staircase, grinning.

Gemma screamed. It was either that or explode. She looked at Dana and clasped her hands in prayer. "Please don't be mad."

Dana was Gemma's one-woman cheering section. She was *so* not mad.

"You've got to hear his reason for laughing at you. It has nothing to do with you, and it's actually pretty funny." Gemma hugged herself and then stretched her arms out wide. Think Maria in *The Sound of Music*, only *even* dorkier. "He's so adorable and sweet and—"

"Enough already," Dana moaned. "All America talks about is going to Japan to visit Danny and now all you're going to talk about is going to England with your new boyfriend. Where the fuck am I gonna go? Brooklyn, to watch Kevin tape season two of *Finding Mr. Mann?*"

"Oh *please*," America drawled. She stood slowly and smiled at Gemma. "She's not mad. She's positively giddy for you. And PS, the binoculars were Dana's idea."

"How else was I supposed to see everything?"

Dana motioned for the girls to follow her into the kitchen and opened the stainless steel refrigerator door. "The one thing binoculars couldn't tell me was if this Joe guy is a good kisser. Because I *am* going to be mad if I'm missing out some hot UK lovin'."

Gemma giggled and collapsed onto a chair. "He's not bad," she replied with a modest shrug. But her lips were still tingling and probably would be for the rest of the night.

"You don't like to kiss and tell. I can respect that." America nodded. She clapped her hands together and wiggled her perfectly tweezed eyebrows. "This calls for a celebration. Let's eat tons of cookies or something. And champagne. Lots of champagne. Or we could go out! I could hire a limo, or a helicopter, or we could—"

"You never offer to go all out when *I* get kissed," Dana whined, poking her head up from the fridge.

"I'm not *that* rich," America teased.

Gemma laughed. "That's really sweet, America, but honestly…" She reached down, slowly easing the Manolos off her aching feet. The blisters were gruesome. "All I want to do is take off these Manolo *fucking* Blahniks and hang out with my two best friends."

"Well, I'll call them," Dana said, pulling a leftover Dutch chocolate cake out of the fridge. "But they may not be able to come over on such short notice."

"Ha-ha," Gemma muttered. "And definitely yes to champagne. Anything to numb the pain while you amputate my feet."

America rustled up three crystal champagne flutes while Dana brought the chocolate cake and an already-chilled bottle of Dom over to the table.

"This cake is awesome," Dana praised with hazy intensity as she dug into it with her bare hands.

Apparently her "no binging" rule was on hiatus.

The girls sat at the breakfast nook devouring chocolate cake, swigging champagne, and giggling about boys. It felt so perfect. A chill went up Gemma's spine as a realization hit her. She was a New Yorker. For two more months anyway. But she wasn't going to stress herself out by thinking about the end of summer already. She took a swig of champagne and grabbed a forkful of cake, giggling as Dana recounted a story about her latest crush—her therapist.

Like we didn't see *that* one coming.

About the Author

Alexandra Richards, twenty-seven, was raised by two successful writers in Santa Fe, New Mexico. She moved to New York to study photography at Bard College and has since worked in filmmaking, theatre, and most recently as a researcher on a syndicated daytime talk show. She lives in Manhattan and makes amateur horror films for fun. Visit her online at www.alexrichards.org.